I0544909

THE SCOTTISH KING

MACBETH AND THE PSYCHOTHERAPIST

A NOVEL

MICHAEL KERR SCOTT

"A fascinating read and an unusual take on the play, the characters and the novel form."
– John Drakakis

EER FICTION
Edward Everett Root, Publishers, Brighton, 2024.

EER FICTION

Edward Everett Root, Publishers Co. Ltd.

Atlas Chambers, 33 West Street, Brighton, BN1 2RE, England

Full details of our stock-holding overseas agents in America, Australia, China, Europe, Japan, and North America, and how to order our books, are given on our website.

We stand with Ukraine. EER books are *not* for sale in Belarus or Russia.

www.eerpublishing.com

edwardeverettroot@yahoo.co.uk

Michael Kerr Scott, *The Scottish King, Macbeth and the Psychotherapist*

© Michael Kerr Scott 2024

First published in England by Edward Everett Root Publishers, 2024.

This edition © Edward Everett Root Publishers 2024.

ISBN 9781915115331 Hardback

ISBN 9781915115607 Paperback

ISBN 9781915115348 ebook

All rights reserved. No part of this publication may be reproduced, stored in a retrieval system or transmitted in any form or by any means, without the prior written permission of the copyright owner.

The right of Michael Kerr Scott to be identified as the author of this work has been asserted in accordance with section 77 of the Copyright, Designs and Patents Act of 1988.

Cover design and book production by Andrew Chapman

www.preparetopublish.com

THE AUTHOR

Michael Scott is a noted theatre critic and lecturer. He is a widely published authority on Shakespeare and on Elizabethan drama. His books include *John Marston's Plays: Theme, Structure and Performance* (Macmillan 1978); *Renaissance Drama and A Modern Audience* (Palgrave Macmillan 1982); *Shakespeare and The Modern Dramatist* (St Martin's Press 1989); Shakespeare, *A Complete Introduction* (John Murray Press, 2017)

He has previously published fiction as Michael Kerr Scott: *Arthur, Legends of the King* (Albert Bridge Books 2017) and *Hamlet and the Psychotherapist: A Novel* (EER Fiction 2022). He is currently a Senior Fellow and the Senior Dean at Blackfriars Hall, Oxford, and Director of the Future of the Humanities Project with Georgetown University, Washington, D.C.

BOOKS BY MICHAEL SCOTT

JOHN MARSTON'S PLAYS: THEME STRUCTURE AND
PERFORMANCE (Macmillan)

RENAISSANCE DRAMA AND A MODERN AUDIENCE
(Macmillan)

SHAKESPEARE AND THE MODERN DRAMATIST
(Macmillan)

THE CHANGELING: A CRITICAL STUDY (Penguin)

ANTONY AND CLEOPATRA: TEXT AND PERFORMANCE
(Macmillan)

SHAKESPEARE'S COMEDIES: ALL THAT MATTERS (Hodder
and Stoughton)

SHAKESPEARE'S TRAGEDIES: ALL THAT MATTERS
(Hodder and Stoughton)

SHAKESPEARE: A COMPLETE INTRODUCTION (John
Murray, Hodder and Stoughton)

As Michael Kerr Scott

TEN STORIES OF KING ARTHUR (FLTR Press, Beijing)

published in the U.K. as:

ARTHUR LEGENDS OF THE KING (Albert Bridge Books)

HAMLET AND THE PSYCHOTHERAPIST: A NOVEL (EER
Fiction)

Edited by Michael Scott

HAROLD PINTER: A CASEBOOK: THE BIRTHDAY PARTY,
THE CARETAKER, THE HOMECOMING (Macmillan)

TALKING SHAKESPEARE (co-edited with Deborah Cartmell)
(Palgrave, Macmillan)

THE TEXT AND PERFORMANCE SERIES (24 volumes)
(Macmillan)

THE CRITICS DEBATE SERIES (22 volumes) (Macmillan)

CHRISTIAN SHAKESPEARE: QUESTION MARK (co-edited
with Michael J Collins) (Vernon Press)

The purpose of playing... is, to hold as 'twere the mirror up to nature; to show virtue her own feature, scorn her own image, and the very age and body of the time his form and pressure.

William Shakespeare, *Hamlet* 3.2: 14-17

To

Margaret and Ted Kennedy

PART I
THE SCOTTISH KING

CHAPTER 1

To get tickets for Sir Ralph Mckenzie's *Macbeth* in London, was no mean achievement. My wife Amelia had phoned the box office some minutes before the lines opened, in order to get a place in the queue. She waited nearly an hour listening to muzak over and over again before being answered, but her patience was rewarded! Two tickets for the opening night. We were so excited. We arrived in plenty of time for the play, but as we got to the theatre, we noticed a commotion outside the stage door. There was an ambulance in attendance and a couple of police cars, with blue lights flashing. The rumour among the crowd was that someone had been run over. Not wishing to miss any part of the performance, we went inside the theatre, bought our programmes, found our seats and waited for the start of the play. There was a delay. All the stage lights came on and a man walked on stage to address us.

"Ladies and gentlemen," he said, "My name is Cornelius Grande and I'm the stage manager for this production of *Macbeth*. Unfortunately, we can't go ahead with tonight's performance, since Sir Ralph has just been involved in an accident outside the stage door and is unable to appear. His understudy, Ben Kelly, told us this afternoon that he has influenza and therefore, the performance has had to be cancelled. Arrangements will be made to refund or exchange your tickets."

The play's production had been billed as the performance of the year, but what was Sir Ralph doing outside the stage door, so soon before the performance was due to start? According to the newspapers the next day, the 'Macbeth Curse' had struck again in the most extraordinary of ways. There are so many superstitions about this play and so many stories of actors going ill, or stages collapsing, or actors falling off the stage, or fire breaking out, that some actors are afraid to even mention the name 'Macbeth'. Instead, they call the drama 'The Scottish Play,' and the protagonist 'The Scottish King', rather than using the 'Macbeth' word. If, by accident, they do mention the name backstage, they have to go through a ritual of turning around three times, leaving the building, swearing, and knocking at a stage door to be allowed re-entry. It's irrational, but many actors take it seriously, no matter how distinguished they might be. Sir Ralph was no exception. He had arrived to prepare for the first night and while backstage, a young female reporter had asked him about the character he was to play. Sir Ralph, rather taken with the attractiveness of the young lady, without thinking said,

"Well, Macbeth you see..."

There was a gasp in the dressing room, up the stairs, across the stage, up to the gantry and around the empty auditorium so that all the seats and the whole edifice itself seemed to shudder. In order to halt any oncoming disaster, Sir Ralph immediately turned round three times and made for the stage door. But as he rushed outside, he was hit by some fool going far too fast on an electric scooter. The great actor fell to the ground and swore. He tried to get up but 'break a leg' is what he had done and now he wasn't even able to rise to knock at the stage door to gain re-entry. The curse had struck again!

There was some speculation in social media as to whether

Sir Ralph when he had recovered, should still knock at the stage door to get into the theatre for a rearranged opening night. Others thought that Sir Ralph should be back on stage as soon as possible, portraying Macbeth with a plastered leg and a crutch, leading to a discussion about Sir Antony Sher's famous portrayal of Richard lll as 'a spider on crutches'. Less sympathetic journalists reported that by breaking a leg he had technically taken his curtain call and that was that for his Scottish King!

What about the poor guy on the scooter? He was photographed visiting Sir Ralph in hospital in order to receive the great actor's forgiveness (and autograph). The photograph was printed in a magazine with an accompanying article suggesting that it was a warning to the country if not the world – but it didn't specify what exactly the warning was about!

I was intrigued by all of this. When did the superstitions about 'the devil's play' arise? You only have to Google 'Macbeth superstitions' to find a series of specific mishaps that have been recorded over the centuries. The Royal Shakespeare Company has even provided a list on its website of the misfortunes that have occurred in many productions at Stratford. History tells us further, that at Astor Place in New York on 10th May 1849, there had been a riot outside the Opera House, prompted by the differing modes of performance between an American actor and a British actor performing Macbeth's role. Twenty-two people were killed by the militia and over a hundred more were injured.

In the late nineteenth century, the critic and caricaturist, Max Beerbohm peddled a story that on the first production of the play in Shakespeare's time the boy playing Lady Macbeth had died, bringing bad luck for future productions.

Sir Ralph would now go down, basking in the glory of being yet another victim of the Scottish curse. I was having none of this malarky! The cancelled performance sparked an inquiry in me. What was causing all of this nonsense about the play? I read the play again and I watched different screen versions of it. The more I saw, the more intrigued I became. It wasn't just the superstitions, but the judgments made about this dark, horrific story of riddles, prophecy, war, witchcraft, misogyny and slaughter. I needed to find out more.

How and why did the superstitions start? Why, after giving out one of the most famous soliloquies in the English language concluding that 'life's a meaningless tale told by an idiot', does the dramatist give the murderer some kind of heroic death? Surely you shouldn't make a hero out of a tyrant, a child murderer, whose last act before fighting Macduff is to kill young Siward in battle? It was all so puzzling. There was more to it than I could find out from the books that talked of ambition or the nature of tragedy. I needed first-hand information. I had to go back to the time it was written.

That might seem a ridiculous idea, but I had done it before over issues relating to *Hamlet* and still had the means to do it, because of an invention by my wife, Dr Amelia Angel. Through a clever use of technology, she could actually move from one time to another. It was a little like the way in which through holography, a pop group such as Abba or The Beatles could be recreated to give a concert years after they had broken up – except, that is achieved by 3D images and recordings of them. In Amelia's technology a living person, not the image, could be transported back in time.

But why should I want to do it? I am Dr Jacob Fortune, a psychotherapist, who over the years, has developed an interest in the theatre. I have studied the way actors find their personal identities woven into the fictional creation of the roles they play. I have no doubt, for example, that if we had seen Sir Ralph in *Macbeth*, he would have become for us the character Macbeth. I have often wondered when, after a great performance, people queue up at the stage door to get autographs, whose autographs do they want? Is it the actor or is it the character that is being portrayed? The two on the stage are as one.

Irrespective of Sir Ralph's misfortune, I wanted to return to Shakespeare's London. Sir Ralph's accident, in raising again the superstitions over *Macbeth*, gave me the perfect reason to justify to Amelia why I should travel to Jacobean London. The last time I was there, Queen Elizabeth I was on the throne, but I wondered what had happened when she had died. What was her successor like? What kind of monarch and man was he, who came down from Scotland to succeed to the English throne? What was this real Scottish King's attitude towards the theatre?

I am a middle-aged man of mixed race and knew the dangers of being what the Jacobeans called "an alien", that is someone from a different country, as opposed to a 'foreigner' who was from a different town! If my wife was in agreement with my travels, she would be able to monitor me, as she does with the other two members of our Practice, *4 Psychotherapists 4 U*, who are currently in Elizabethan England. She is our anchor in the 21st century and has an array of devices for keeping us in touch with her, but unfortunately, not with each other. That was a technology on which she was still engaged. Using Amelia's means of travel I could return.

When I was last in Elizabethan London, I had established a profitable branch, *4P4U,* which specialised in providing 'talking therapy', particularly for those in the acting profession and in the government circles in England. I had been replaced in that Elizabethan practice by my twin sister, Dr Jackie Fortune, whose hair and clothing were such that she could be mistaken for me. Especially, as the first thing that some white people notice about us is our skin colour, followed by the comment, 'But you all look the same.'

She had taken my name, Dr Jacob Fortune, for several reasons.

Firstly, she was in love with my former lover in the 21st century, Dr Ever Truslove, who insisted on being a non-binary, no-pronoun person. The London of Elizabeth 1 had clearly not been ready for such a character, so Ever, being there with Jackie, had reluctantly identified as female.

Therein lay the second issue – society in the seventeenth century did not recognise the existence of a conjugal relationship between two women. Only the existence of such a relationship between two men was acknowledged and that was condemned and punished by execution, unless of course, you happened to be of the 'right' social status. A woman who 'exaggeratedly' behaved outside the expectations of the male-dominated society, however, could be branded as a witch and as such executed. A woman loving another woman was clearly outside these expectations and therefore the relationship was not recognised! So, if Ever were a woman, Jackie had to be a man and she consequently took my name and sex.

Thirdly, at that time, females were rarely allowed to be doctors of any kind, as Shakespeare has helpfully reminded us in *All's Well That Ends Well*. In the 21st century Jackie and Ever were Doctors in Clinical Psychology, just as I am.

Jackie soon felt fairly secure in the disguise of her gender, in common with Shakespeare's Rosalind, when she was Ganymede in *As You Like It*, or Viola when she was Cesario in *Twelfth Night*. Indeed, Ever had been taken on by Shakespeare's theatre company, The Lord Chamberlain's Men, to instruct the boy actors on how they could be one sex, disguised as another and yet pretending to be the first.

But to which year should I return to get answers about *Macbeth*? The play, apparently, had one of its first performances in 1606 at Hampton Court Palace, which the real Scottish King (who was also the new King of England) and his brother-in-law the Danish King, attended. The problem was that no evidence was available of that performance. Why do we have no record of it? What happened? Did the superstition about the play arise during or after that performance? These for me were interesting questions for which I might get an answer but only if I went back in time. There would be no point, however, in just going back to 1606. I needed to find out more about the background and build up to that performance. Something weird or extraordinary may have taken place. It was locked in history and I was determined to unlock it.

I thought that the death of Queen Elizabeth 1 would be a good place to start, so back in our consulting rooms, I decided to approach Amelia about my desire to return to 1603. After a long discussion, she finally agreed that I could do so.

We went into the office where Dafydd, our practice manager, was sitting at his desk, trying to organise our appointments and paperwork. It included getting locums or part-time staff to replace us when we were away. Dafydd looked up at us and complained, "Keeping track of you lot is like herding cats." He then told us that Jackie and Ever had been advised by Augustine Phillips, the theatre manager of the Elizabethan Globe Theatre, who had helped me on my last visit, that they should leave London because he was worried about the possibility of riots when Queen Elizabeth died.

Augustine felt that Jackie, whom he thought was me, Jacob, was particularly vulnerable being of colour. You see as twins we are both of mixed race and thereby of colour! Augustine therefore had made arrangements for Jacob (i.e. Jackie) and Ever to stay with friends of the theatre, called Davenant, who took in lodgers at the Salutation Tavern in Oxford. For me that was perfect. There would be no chance of the two 'Jacobs' being together in the consulting room in Elizabethan London, so I could return there to start my new adventure.

Dafydd was about to tell me more when his wife Maddie, who also worked in our office, came in with Spikey their cat, who was in his bag-shaped carrier.

"You don't mind Spikey coming in do you?" she said. "He's not found many mice lately so I thought he might try his luck around here."

"No, no." I replied, "Dafydd was just saying…"

"Well, you see," interrupted Maddie letting the cat out of

the bag, "I've just been to the doctor," and turning to Dafydd she said, "We are going to have a baby!"

"What!" Dafydd exclaimed and he ran to her and hugged her.

Amelia and I congratulated the happy couple, told them that I was returning to Elizabethan London and then gave them the rest of the day off while we sorted things out in the office.

Dafydd shook his head in despair at my news but he thanked us and the excited couple went off, leaving the cat and its carrier with us.

"Well Jacob, when are you intending to return?" I took a deep breath and said that there was no time like the present and so I'd better get ready.

I went into the Practice's bathroom and looked at the large mirror that was hanging between the wash basin and the shower. I always thought it was too large and at one time in trying to remove it, I had cracked it slightly. Amelia had been furious.

"Don't you know, that breaking a mirror is unlucky?"

"I haven't broken it," I had replied, "I just cracked it a little at the top corner."

"Don't mess with it again," she had said, "We don't want bad luck for the next seven years!"

"Bad luck! We're psychotherapists, we don't believe in bad luck."

"Well, I do," she had said, "At least as far as mirrors are concerned." At the time we both laughed at the absurdity of it.

In looking at myself in that mirror now, I started to think about what I was taking on. Psychotherapists, I suppose, shouldn't talk to themselves, but I was talking to my reflection.

"Jacob," I said, "You look as if your enthusiasm for inquiry is going to get you into another adventure. I wonder if being of colour will turn out to be a problem, especially if the riots do break out. There were people of colour in Elizabethan and

Jacobean England, and you didn't have a lot of trouble when you were there before, but you'll need to take care." I gave myself a wink.

"It's all very well you winking at me," the reflection replied, "but if you get the plague, which you know from history is about to break out again in Shakespeare's London, you'll not see me again," I assured my reflection that everything would be fine. "If plague breaks out, I'll make sure to leave London!" I said the words slowly so I could lip-read my reflection.

I dressed in the Elizabethan clothes that I had used on the last visit and was ready. I knew that Maddie would send more clothes in a couple of days. In fact, they might even arrive before I did – such were the vagaries of this form of travel. But that's the virtue of this system – you play around with time.

I turned back to the mirror and repeated,

"You play around with time. Don't you agree? I mean, if I could do it with you now, in the mirror, I might even be able to get rid of that pesky crack."

I don't know why I then did what I did, but I gave the crack a tap with the end of my electric razor. With horror, it started to grow across the whole of the glass. Then the glass fell to the floor in a tremendous crash.

"Oh no," I said, as I heard a knocking at the bathroom door.

"What's going on?" It was Amelia and I was in trouble.

"Come in," I shouted, "It's the mirror." She saw the pieces of mirror all around my feet, reflecting numerous images of me, like a broken jigsaw.

"Take care, that you don't cut yourself."

"I thought you'd be angry," I said, as I gingerly made my way across the room to her.

"Angry? Why should I be angry?"

"Because I've broken the mirror."

"No, no, you don't understand. You've done that twice now,

which means your bad luck will go and your good luck will return."

"Are you just making that up?" I asked.

"Probably, but I wanted you to feel good before you leave. You could have smashed it with a hammer for all I care because then I don't have to think about your clumsiness when I see that crack!". We laughed and held each other tight and then we walked back into my consulting room. Amelia had set the coordinates and my journey began.

Would my new adventure be like a reflection, a dream, or a nightmare? Would I find the answers to my discontent with this dark, bloody play, *Macbeth*, written in the reign of a new Scottish King? Maybe the new Scottish King was part of the mystery of the play.

CHAPTER 2

I had planned to arrive inside the *4P4U* consulting room, located in Elizabethan London, but I came down with a splash in a rather large puddle in an alleyway just around the corner from it. No sooner had I come to my senses, than a black ball of fluff dropped into my lap with a howl. I turned on the torch on my watch.

"Good God!" I said, "What are you doing here, Spikey?" Maddie's cat, who had never liked me much, just stared at me as if to say,

"What the hell have you got me into this time?"

"Don't look at me like that!" I said, "I'm the one who's wet."

Spikey must have crept into the portal when Maddie let him out of his basket. He had come with me the last time I journeyed to Elizabethan London and it seems he had travelled reluctantly with me this time.

I stood up and both Spikey and I wrinkled our noses at the smell of sewage and rotten food that I remembered from last time. With Spikey keeping close to me, we made our way down the alley, round the corner towards the consulting room. It was midnight and I felt trepidation as I reached the door. The door was locked but I opened it with the key, which we kept for emergencies in a safe place. Spikey darted in, making for his old sleeping place beneath a cupboard. The room was tidy and everything looked neat and professional. Indeed, it was far tidier than I had ever had it, but that would have been down to Jackie. I was sorry that I wouldn't be seeing Jackie and Ever.

I sat down in my brown leather chair and fell asleep

I was woken up by someone shaking me.

"Jacob, are you ill? Where is Ever? Why are you still here?" I recognised the voice of my old friend from the Globe Theatre, Augustine Phillips. Obviously, he thought I was Jackie who had become Jacob after my last visit.

"Augustine," I said, There's no problem. I just fell asleep. Ever has gone to Oxford by coach ahead of me. I'm staying here for a while longer."

"That's good then," Augustine said. "I was passing and I saw your door open and thought something was wrong. But I must rush, lots to do at the theatre. I will talk to you later." As he left the room, he told me that there were crowds around that day. It seemed as if everyone was making their way to the Cathedral. With that, he dashed off up the road towards the Globe.

"Well Spikey," I said. "At least there is one person here that I know." Spikey had also found a companion – or was it just food? He dropped a mouse at my feet and looked up at me with pride.

I decided to seek out Jackie and Ever's lodgings at The Elephant, where I had previously stayed, but first I picked up my large, old water jug and went out to buy some fresh water, brought from upstream in boats and sold on the riverbank, next to the stinking Thames. I saw that Augustine was right about the crowds crossing the bridge or taking the ferry boats, heading towards the city.

As I walked towards The Elephant, I noticed that the doors were open, but the manager, Richard Wisely, was nowhere to be seen. I went up the first flight of stairs to the rooms that Jackie and Ever rented. I noticed some of Ever's clothes strewn around the closet, while all of Jackie's were neatly folded away. I looked out of the window and saw the crowds gathering on the bridge. Something was going on and I felt the inquisitor's need to find out what it was. Maybe the Queen had died. How long had I been travelling? The coordinates had been set by Amelia on my request so that I would arrive before the Queen's death. I drank some of the fresh water and left.

It was a cold blustery day. I went to join the crowd making their way across London Bridge. People were pushing and jostling each other since the centre of the bridge was obstructed by a line of stationary carts. Up ahead, Officers of the Crown had requisitioned a cart of winter vegetables, not for their consumption, but because the cart was required for government business. The cart owner had been roughly evicted from his transport and lay flat on the ground amongst the vegetables which had been dispatched on top of him. The newly acquired horse and vehicle were on their way toward St. James's Palace. The other horses on the bridge were a little restless, occasionally relieving themselves, which meant that I had to pick my way carefully along the road.

I learned from the people around me that everyone was heading towards St Paul's Cathedral.

"What's going on?" I asked.

"The execution, of course, it's going to be a big show."

I was curious so I continued walking with the crowd and saw a huge gallows that had been set up in the Cathedral grounds. It was large enough to hang 6 victims at a time.

A couple of women got into conversation with me, saying in rough, excited voices,

"The Cathedral always attracts a good audience for a big execution!" They wanted to see the kicking, dancing, ejaculation, castration, and 'opening up' of the 'criminals' concerned. "But today the show will be better than usual," one of them exclaimed and she went on to say that there was a 'special event' as they would see not just three men but also three women, notorious witches, being hanged simultaneously. Three women and three men, swaying in the wind, before being gutted on the stage. One of the men was the father of one of the others, the third was a petty criminal who had stolen some barley. This was an entertainment that the Elizabethan audience could not wait to see.

There was no going back through the crowd for me since I was literally pushed towards the execution ground, finishing on a bank that ironically had a good view of the scene. The three witches were already tied to posts. They had not been drawn through the streets, behind horses from Newgate prison, but had been conveyed in a cart. They, of course, had done a deal with their jailers, promising them the only thing that they had, which was their bodies. If they hadn't done so willingly, they may have been raped anyway but they had given the jailers a good time and were recompensed after a fashion. On their journey, they had been pelted with stones, mud, dung and rotten fruit. Taunts and curses had been shouted at them, but at least their flesh had not been torn apart by the rough stones on the road. It was different for the three men, who had been tied onto pallets and raced through the streets. They arrived at the Cathedral, bruised, bloodied and broken. They were cheered and jeered as they were led to the posts and tied up. The aim of the executioner was to get his six victims hanging, naked in a row. Sometimes women would have had sacks tied at their waists to catch 'seepage' as they hung. But not today, as the executioner wanted to 'let their women's innards come out.' This was going to be as gruesome as a sport could be. The aim of the victims, however, was a little different.

The petty thief, who had stolen the barley for his family, was the first to be taken and noosed. As the rope was placed around his neck, he was lowered from the gallows and was left hanging in the wind as the noose tightened. The boy was to be next so that his father would see him struggle as the noose started to choke him. But the father shed no tears. He had instructed the boy as to what to do. As the lad was forced up the ladder to the gallows bridge and the noose put around his neck, his father shouted out 'Now'. The executioner turned and the boy jumped, hanging limp in the noose with his neck broken. The pain would have been minimal. There was a gasp from the audience and then someone started to clap at the bravery of the lad and the crowd cheered. His mother, watching on, had screamed and fallen into the arms of one of her friends. The father then was beaten and dragged to the ladder, but as he climbed it the three witches, who had been watching silently, began a rapid, low incantation, which gradually became louder and louder. The executioner's assistants instructed them to be quiet, but still, they continued to chant. They began stamping their feet and pulling at their ropes. The executioner was distracted again and the father, in imitation of his son, threw himself from the gallows and so broke his neck and died like his child.

Everything was going wrong with the great performance. A stronger wind had now got up, as if in answer to the witches' incantation and a black thundercloud covered the sky. Lightning flashed and torrential rain began to fall so that people had to run for shelter. The executioner descended from his ladder and ran towards the Cathedral. Some men in the crowd took the ladder and raised it to the thief's body which was violently swinging from the neck. It was too late as the wind had done for him. They then looked around for the witches, but they had disappeared into the crowd or as some said, 'into the wind'. All the preparations for the disembowelling of the victims had been blown to the ground, so terrible was the storm. The thief's body, as with that of the father and son, was taken away in all the confusion. The executioner was left with nothing for which he could claim his expenses. Some days later I heard that the same executioner was himself executed in the grounds of Newgate Prison. He was not disembowelled as it was decided it wasn't really his fault, but he had nevertheless failed in his duty.

There was much talk about the witches – were they so powerful as to summon the storm and then vanish themselves? People reckoned that the women had cried out to Hecate, the witches' goddess, and her supernatural animals – the toad Paddock and the cat Gray-Malkin – to come to their aid. The talk in the crowd was that they were witches right enough, as only witches can entirely disappear like that. No one saw where they went or how they went. They just vanished.

What did all this portend? Rumour and superstition were rife and people were asking, whether the Queen was about to die. She had not been seen for many weeks and was apparently at Richmond. Some said that there had been a number of Scotsmen wearing kilts at the executions. Had they been sent by the Scottish King to find out if the Queen had died? The Scottish King was himself a notorious witch hunter. Who were the father and son being executed? Were they more important than anyone had imagined? Was the other man just a common thief?

It was rumoured that there had been a disagreement between Sir Walter Raleigh and Robert Cecil, the Queen's Chief Minister, over who should succeed Elizabeth when she died. But it was against the law to speculate. The Earl of Essex had led one rebellion, which had got him executed. A supporter of Essex, Henry Wriothesley, the Earl of Southampton, was still in the Tower for his involvement in that rebellion. Essex was dead but why was Southampton still alive? Was he to be the next King? Was he in league with the witches?

A cry of "Shush, mind what you're saying there might be spies about," echoed around me. The Scottish King had no time for witch-sympathisers. In Scotland, he had such women burned, just on the suspicion of being witches.

"Shush, wait for any announcements," I was told.

There were cries of, "If the Queen is dead what will people do?" "Will there be rioting gangs of youths?" "Will they go through the streets destroying, maiming, killing?" "Who will be in charge to stop them?" "God save the Queen." "God help us deal with witchcraft." "God take care of me and mine."

When I got back to my consulting room, I decided to write down my thoughts in a journal. I needed to try and make sense of what was happening around me. Was the seventeenth century so different from the twenty-first century? Were these people very different from those in my own time?

JOURNAL

I had been sickened by what I had witnessed. There had been a 'blood-lust' within the crowd as they went in expectation of the performance of the executioner. They had wanted to see the cruelty of it all but then the weather had intervened. Some thought that it had been at the command of the witches and that was why it all went so wrong for the executioner.

How fickle crowds are! I am aware that this wasn't something peculiar to Elizabethan times. In Roman times people paid money to watch miscreants being fed to wild animals. Back home, in the 20th century, in the United States, the Ku Klux Klan hanged black people with crowds urging them on. In the 21st century, executions in the Middle East have been filmed and shown in the media.

This is an unhealthy trait within the psyche of humans when they can enjoy the pain and death of others. We still live in the shadow of the Holocaust and its aftermath. We watch as war rages around the world. For most of us, it is news, but for a few, it is the gratification of an interest in violence and obscenity.

CHAPTER 3

A fter all I had witnessed, what was I going to do now? I felt as if I were in the first act of a play, but I had no script. Rather like the actors in the plays at the Globe who, in those days, also had no scripts. Most of them were given their roles, on rolls of paper, which contained their cues and their particular lines for them to commit to memory, even when doubling up on parts. They'd only get a full knowledge of the play concerned when acting their roles together with other actors. At this moment in my personal 'play' I was on the stage alone.

I fleetingly saw the so-called witches again not long after their escape. They peered in the window of my consulting room as they passed along the street. I looked up and they were gone. Spikey had seen them, arched his back and then ran under the cupboard. It was quite off-putting.

A few minutes later, I thought I heard someone at the door and I opened it. There was a black cat standing on the doorstep ready to enter. Suddenly Spikey darted out from under the cupboard and puffing out his fur, he hissed at the would-be intruder. The other cat's back went up in response. Then someone called out and the animal ran off in the direction of the river. Spikey looked at me as if to say,

"Don't trust that feline, she's not good news." I laughed and bent down to stroke him.

"I'm not superstitious Spikey," I said, "Not even about black cats, since you are one yourself." Spikey seemed to understand and returned to his place under the cupboard, clearly satisfied that he had helped me avoid some disaster or other. I watched him with a smile on my face and then turned back to close the door.

"I wondered whether you were going to shut the door on me," Augustine shouted, as he pushed past me into the room.

"I was distracted by the cat," I retorted.

"Cats are for outdoors not indoors, as I've told you many times," he replied,

"Not my cat," I said, "He has a flea collar on, which helps to keep him clean."

"Nonsense," Augustine said. "Whoever told you that saw an innocent to con." He paused and then told me that he had just heard that the Queen had died and that the odds were that the King of Scotland would be the next King of England.

"What do you think that would mean for the company?" I asked. He said that we'd have to wait and see, adding with a sigh that,

"Reportedly the King of Scotland likes extravaganzas and masques more than plays, just as he likes hunting more than working."

I questioned him on whether there were any other contenders for the Monarchy. He replied that Sir Walter Raleigh, who had been such a favourite of the Queen, preferred another candidate, Arabella Stuart, but Augustine's money was on Robert Cecil getting his own way by having the Scottish King acclaimed.

The theatre had to have its ear to the ground and I knew

that Augustine was likely to be right. I learned later that as soon as Elizabeth had died, Cecil had instructed a rider to go as fast as possible to Edinburgh and meet with the King of Scotland. He was to greet him as the new King of England. Unbelievably, it took the rider only three days to make the journey, which led to the suspicion that perhaps Cecil had pre-empted the Queen's death. Meanwhile, across London and the rest of the country, Cecil had arranged for the news of Queen Elizabeth's death to be announced, together with the announcement that the Scottish King was the new King of England. Raleigh and other opponents had been completely outmanoeuvred by the speed of Cecil's organisation.

I realised that the reign of the Tudors was over. That dynasty had caused several problems with Spain. There was Henry Vlll's divorce from his long-standing and faithful Spanish wife Catherine of Aragon. That 'poor lady' was at rest in Peterborough Cathedral. Later Elizabeth had rejected the idea of marrying the King of Spain, who had been the husband of her sister, Queen Mary Tudor. Tension with Spain had resulted in hostilities throughout Elizabeth's reign. Raleigh, although a Protestant, thought that perhaps Arabella Stuart could bring a reconciliation between the nations, but Cecil needed to control the new Monarch and he believed that he could do that with the Scotsman. Cecil knew the Scottish King was one who liked attention but not work. Robert Cecil would be the man behind the throne. With this Scot as King, he would have more power than either his father, William Cecil, or even Francis Walsingham had enjoyed under Queen Elizabeth. Cecil had decided that he must prove to be invaluable to the new, proud, self-indulgent Monarch.

Apparently, on hearing the news of the Queen's death, the Scottish King had immediately started on a well-planned procession through England to London. He went from town to town, county to county, distributing his largesse. His wife, with whom he was not well pleased, stayed behind, as did his eldest son Henry, over whom they constantly argued. Once the King had left Scotland, the determined Queen arranged that she and her son would come to London as soon as possible.

The new King made his way through England where the population welcomed him, with his proclamation to open up the prisons and free all except traitors and murderers. He let everyone know that whatever their faith, they could practise it without penalty under his new regime. This last point, however, was something that hadn't been agreed with Cecil. On hearing it, Cecil decided it would have to be withdrawn. The new King had been declaring religious tolerance but if he tolerated the rich Catholic landowners, who were heavily fined monthly for sticking to the Old Faith, the exchequer would suffer. Wealthy Catholics ironically meant a wealthy Monarchy. Cecil had put the Scottish King on the English throne and therefore the Monarch felt that Cecil could be trusted. Perhaps, the King hadn't meant religious toleration in a sustained way! Indeed, there had been enough tolerance already. The fines were to remain and it was decreed that he had never promised a policy of religious freedom, not even inadvertently!

What of the witches, I wondered, a favourite subject of the new Monarch? In Scotland, he had ruled that witches should be burned. Pyres were common and shrewish women, who were vociferous in their opinions, were likely to be assigned to the flames. In England, however, they were hanged or drowned. There was no need to change that protocol for Hecate's 'army'. In some towns, the witches were lifted high into the air on instruments made especially for the spectacle. They were left there for hours, even days, suspended over a river or a lake. If they survived, it was proclaimed that they must be witches and therefore they would be plummeted into the water and drowned. If they had died, they were obviously innocent and had been taken into the care of God. Any shrewish woman might be labelled a witch by those wanting to rid themselves of her. Such was the nonsense of the rule of law.

When the Scottish King eventually arrived near London, at the Theobalds Estate, owned by Robert Cecil, he found it a most attractive place. Although, whilst in Scotland, he hadn't been sure whether to trust Cecil, he found that the Estate of the Chief Minister was excellent for hunting. Cecil arranged that, before the King proceeded into London, the Privy Council should come and stay, as his guests, at the estate. They decided that they needed to get the Queen's funeral out of the way before the new Monarch entered the city.

While the Scottish King hunted deer on Cecil's estate, Cecil and the Privy Council returned to London to bury the Queen, who had lain in state in her ornate coffin for long enough. Sir Walter Raleigh, her friend and favourite, was still full of himself. He believed that after the funeral, he would at least become Governor of Jersey or better still, gain some even greater title like Essex before him. However, he would have to pay the ultimate price for his popularity, if he were seen as a threat to the King and thereby to Cecil. To put it in the vernacular, Cecil was a cunning puppeteer, pulling strings and then letting them go, whilst the Scottish King hunted, caroused and drank, thinking that he himself was the puppeteer.

JOURNAL

How strange it was. I had come from an England where political puppeteers were promising favours or threatening obscurity if the puppets whom they wanted to control didn't do what they demanded. In the contemporary world, it is usually the mandarins of a political party and the very wealthy who wield the power and pull the strings while other politicians and bosses dance to the tune of honours and government contracts. But in Cecil's time, he was in charge.

The 1603 plague has started to appear and I'm not sure how I'll cope with it, nor know how the government will act. But certainly, as far as the King is concerned, he wants to keep out of the city for as long as possible, only entering briefly and then going back to safety. The start of the plague was already playing into Cecil's hands. He was exploiting it to gain more power. This is just like the 21st century when COVID was being exploited by those in power to make more money for their friends and families.

CHAPTER 4

The state funeral of Elizabeth 1 was set for the 28th April 1603, after a month of lying in state. There was a lot to do but Cecil was confident enough that Raleigh would ensure the funeral procession would go well and that the Abbey would sort out the service appropriately. Some of the boy actors at the Globe had been choristers at St Paul's and so they were drafted into the Abbey choir. This put a strain on the company. Before she had left for Oxford, my colleague Ever had been training the boy actors for the various female roles in *Twelfth Night* and a new play *Troilus and Cressida*, which was to go into repertory after the funeral.

I knew this new play to be quite bitter. Would it reflect a change already within the country which might lack stability now that the Queen had died? Many had expected that the new King would be tolerant of different faiths, but they were to be disappointed. Cecil thought he was managing the transition well but there was already rancour brewing in the country at large. It was also evident that the plague was returning – "A plague on both your houses," – was a line from *Romeo and Juliet*, a play which had appeared after an earlier plague year. To what extent had it been applicable to the House of Tudor and now to the House of Stuart? People believed that the British monarchy was stable and would last for generations and that it could withstand the plagues.

The day before the funeral I noticed, as I walked back to the lodgings at The Elephant, that a strange quiet had descended on the city. Everything seemed peaceful. The Thames was flowing lazily and even London Bridge wasn't as active as usual as many of the shops had ceased trading for the final days of national mourning. Some spiked heads of the executed were silhouetted against the evening sky. But I began to feel a sense of unease about what was to follow now that the Queen was dead. I wondered about what was happening at home with the second Queen Elizabeth who was close to death. How long would she last after 70 years of reign? There was something 'awry in the heavens' but I managed to put such superstitions to one side. I recalled Amelia and the bathroom mirror and shook my head as I laughed at myself. Surely, it can't be bad luck to break a mirror?

On entering The Elephant, there was no sign of the owner, Richard Wisely, and so silently I ascended the stairs to the lodgings. Whilst outside the door, I heard a shuffling in the room but rather than cry out for help, I grasped the handle and barged in. I was startled to see a man at my bedroom table.

"Who are you?" I shouted. "And what are you doing here?" He looked up from the papers he had been reading and calmly replied,

"Shouldn't I be asking you, who you might be?"

"That is none of your business. I think you should leave."

"I may be back." He retorted menacingly as he came towards me.

"Richard," I yelled, as the man went past me and out through the door. I heard Richard coming down the stairs from the second floor. He looked at the man, who then disappeared down the stairs.

Richard ran after him, but the intruder had left the tavern before he could catch him. Richard then came back up to me. "Good fortune that you didn't kill him." He smiled and said that he would secure the doors.

"He was looking through the papers on the table," I said. "And look over there. He has gone through Ever's clothes." But I noticed that Jackie's sober attire was still neatly folded. Richard's eye twitched as he commented that Government agents were everywhere. It didn't mean that I was important – just a curiosity.

Augustine arrived looking very pleased with himself as he had arranged for the two of us to go to the funeral of the Queen, thanks to his connections at court.

The next day, we watched the funeral procession from a good vantage point. The Queen's coffin was laid in a chariot, drawn by four grey horses harnessed in black. The coffin was covered with a purple cloth and on top was a remarkably life-like effigy of Queen Elizabeth l, royally attired. The crowds, which like the procession, included every stratum of society, came out to see it pass by. It was as if the world were in mourning.

Augustine had gained us entry into the Abbey. We were towards the back, but he pointed out Lancelot Andrewes, telling me that he was a leading theologian and Dean of the Abbey. As such, he had responsibility for the funeral service. However, the most important, but now ageing cleric was easy to identify by his sombre finery. Augustine whispered that he was John Whitgift, the Archbishop of Canterbury. This cleric, some years earlier, had ordered the burning of poems and satires by Shakespeare's friend John Marston. I remembered that I had once met Marston's father when I was last here, but I did not meet the young poet and dramatist himself, who perhaps was not just a friend but a protégé of Shakespeare. Augustine peered around the congregation and stifled a laugh. He had spotted young Marston much closer to the proceedings than we were. He pointed to a man with a mop of red hair and said,

"Typical of Marston to get a better place than us, but he is with Shakespeare."

We both looked and saw a man next to the red-headed one but I couldn't see him clearly.

"So that is Marston, the fearless satirist?" Remembering my history, I said to myself, 'You are going the get into real trouble with the incoming King!' I said nothing to Augustine about this, nor about the fact that Archbishop Whitgift, some conjectured, had been in a 'close relationship' with a former Vice Chancellor of Cambridge University, Andrew Perne, who was now dead. The hypocrisy of the situation was interesting – the elite could get away with any sort of sexual/loving behaviour whilst simultaneously condemning it in others, even to the point of having them executed in the grounds of St Paul's Cathedral, not far from the Abbey where we were sitting. Did these supposedly great people project their own illicit behaviours onto others so that they could relieve themselves of the guilt that they felt? Or was it to distract people from their behaviour?

John Marston had been punished for satirising people in power. He was unafraid. "Let Custards quake, my rage must freely runne," he had once stated, adding that he would rant at whoever he wished, especially those whom he considered to be hypocrites in the Church.

Augustine pointed out other players and poets, who were further back than Marston. I wondered how the young satirist had managed to get so close. Perhaps he was deliberately trying to annoy Whitgift who, when he was addressing the congregation, must have seen him. Smirking, Marston looked around at the congregation, then back at Whitgift, as if letting him know that he knew his 'secret'!

The choral music was sublime and the whole ceremony appropriate in its dignity and solemnity. Some of the crowd outside were crying. Others were merely blank-faced. It was a privilege to be there to see it all.

Although later, the Scottish King built a monument for Queen Elizabeth, which can still be seen in the Abbey, she was first laid to rest under the monument of her grandfather Henry Vll. The Scottish King was to have her placed on top of her sister Queen Mary Tudor, as a memorial to them both – Elizabeth on top of Mary. I wonder if he knew how much they disliked each other in life, especially as they had different religious persuasions. I expect he did, but perhaps they would find reconciliation in death! Opposite that monument, which still has the effigy of Elizabeth, the King built a white marble monument to his mother, Mary Queen of Scots. Her body was brought to London from Peterborough Cathedral, where it had been buried. The monument was larger than that of Elizabeth's. Size matters for these vain aristocrats. Most of them spent their lives fearful of losing power, judging others and spreading fear by having any subjects whom they believed were a threat to them, flogged, racked, tortured, executed and butchered.

But all this I knew from history and was bringing it to mind at the actual funeral of the Queen, and in later discussions back at The Elephant or at the theatre with Augustine and in Wilkins Tavern, not far from the Globe, which I often frequented.

As I came out of the Abbey, I caught a glimpse of my intruder in the crowd.

"Do you know who that is?" I asked Augustine, trying to point him out. But when I looked back, the man had disappeared. "I wonder if I'm being watched?"

"Watched?" Augustine replied. "Nonsense! Who would watch you?"

"Thank you," I said and he laughed.

JOURNAL

Both in the 17th century at the funeral of Queen Elizabeth I and in the 21st century at the funeral of Queen Elizabeth II, people jockeyed for position to be closest to the coffin. The nearer to the coffin you were the more important you considered yourself to be.

"Don't worry," I thought, "One day you'll be in one of those and that's the final measure of your importance."

What fools they are. 'Great' men and women believe that they can behave as they want, whilst imposing restrictions on the behaviour of others. In the time of Elizabeth I and the Scottish King, leading men of influence lived together and no doubt were in homosexual relationships, whilst in the rest of the population it was sought out and condemned. Those caught in such a relationship were arrested and some were executed, even in the grounds of the Cathedral or indeed at the doors of the parish churches. Whitgift, for all his intelligence, importance and clerical pomp, appeared to me to be nothing more than an old hypocrite who had ruined many lives, however much he might be held in awe or respect within high society.

Hypocrisy was no different in the 21st century. Whilst illegal drugs were being used by certain Members of Parliament, members of the public were arrested and prosecuted for the same behaviour.

CHAPTER 5

Augustine had fears about possible rioting after the Queen's death but so far these had fortunately not materialised in any dangerous way. However, that didn't mean that people of mixed race like me were safe. The discrimination against people of colour was one of fear, but also one of superstition. Black was the devil's colour and for some, people of colour were his followers. Sometimes people would bump into me 'accidentally' to touch my hand or face, or they would let their children do it, as they wanted to feel my brown flesh. I'd smile and if appropriate shake their hands. But some would run away from 'that darkie' or 'the devil's man'. The roaming gangs of youths would 'eye' me as I passed and maybe shout an obscenity or two, such as 'dirty', or 'brownie', as a greeting. These I would ignore, but now that the Queen was dead, I could be in danger of more than insults, with the instability brought about just by the change of Monarchy.

The young apprentices of the city had little to do after work and so they used to gather in gangs in various places. I tried to keep clear of these. Anyone who was different was a target and had to be careful.

When gangs of lads started to meet at the riverside, close to

The Elephant, alarm bells rang for Richard Wisely, the owner. What could he do about it? They were threatening in their manner and so he tried moving them on, but they mocked him, swore and cursed him for keeping a 'house of aliens'. I, of course, was the only 'guest of colour'. I considered leaving the tavern and heading back to my consulting room to sleep, but Richard thought that we were not in danger and that eventually, the gangs would move away. But they didn't.

One particular day, the lads had been drinking and were deliberately heading for The Elephant to cause trouble. Richard called up to me to stay in my room and lock the door. Meanwhile, he was trying to lock the main door, but it burst open. I went into the closet and backed myself against the wall, listening quietly. I heard my bedroom door crash open and at least two people came in and started rummaging through the room. I heard other loud footsteps continuing up the stairs. The door to the closet was kicked open against me. I grabbed it and held it fast so that it hid me. One of the rioters noticed the clothes inside and shouted,

"Just look at this lot!" He grabbed an armful of Ever's clothes and took them back into the bedroom. There was much hilarity about the style and colour of them. I remained flat against the wall as I heard someone ask,

"Any more?" My heart raced but the reply came,

"Nothing good. We'll take these as there's nothing else round 'ere."

With that, I heard footsteps retreating from the room. I listened to them going up to the second floor in search of better booty. I slid down the wall, shaking with fear and relief. I stayed rooted to the spot, until about 30 minutes later I heard the rioters grimly laughing and shouting as they ran back downstairs and made their way out of the tavern. When I was sure they had left, I tentatively went downstairs and found Richard lying on the floor. He had been punched and kicked, while his tavern had been ransacked. He was lying in a pool of ale, which was coming from some barrels that had been mindlessly smashed open. I noticed some of Ever's clothes had been dropped on the floor as the rioters had moved on, not bothering about what they had left. The incident itself was their excitement.

Richard was still breathing and I helped him as best I could. He was bleeding profusely from a gash on the head. I staunched it with one of Ever's dropped garments, which I ripped up and wound around his head as a bandage. As he slowly came to, he complained about his chest. No doubt a rib or two had been fractured but I surmised that his lungs had not been punctured as he was starting to breathe more steadily. I asked him if there was anyone else in the tavern. He said that there was only Molly, one of the maids, who had a room in the attic. His son Sam was away and there were no guests as they hadn't yet returned from work. My heart sank as I went upstairs.

I found Molly. She had obviously been molested, and her throat had been cut. Who was she and what had she done to deserve to die like this? I came down again and tended to Richard. If that mob had found me, I doubt if I would have been any more alive than Molly was.

I stayed with Richard, looking after him as best I could. I told him about Molly's death. Crying, he asked me to see her. Upstairs, I closed her frightened eyes, cleansed her face covered her neck with one of Ever's scarves and laid her out as best I could. I dressed her in some of Ever's clothes, which had been left in the closet. They were brightly coloured garments. You might even say 'extravagantly so' and Molly would never have worn such finery before. If anyone commented, I would simply tell them that they were clothes made for the theatre. I only knew Molly in death, but I tried to make her as much a 'Queen' as anyone else who had died recently.

Later that evening some of the other guests returned. They were immediately suspicious of me, but luckily Richard was well enough to explain who I was and how I had been looking after him. I told them what had happened to Molly. Two of them rushed upstairs and when they returned, clearly distressed, they thanked me for making her look so pretty. They undertook to inform the authorities.

That night, I returned to my consulting room. The area now seemed quiet. Augustine was waiting for me. The outside door had been broken, furniture upended and books had been thrown around. We straightened up as much as we could. I was just concerned that the fragile electricity was still working so I went outside to check that the solar panels on the roof, which had been put in place when the consulting room came originally from the 21st century, were still intact. They were, so I sent a message back to Amelia, telling her that I'd had some trouble here. I was well but not feeling very safe. I said that the apprentices attacked The Elephant and the consulting room. A serving girl had been murdered. I would decide later what to do.

I learned from Augustine that some of the other taverns had also been attacked by mobs including Wilkins Tavern and brothel where, on my last visit I had also taken lodgings, but no one else had been murdered.

Augustine was concerned about me and wanted me to stay at his home but I thought that was too risky for him and argued that I would be fine staying the night in the consulting room.

Once he had gone, I sent another message to Amelia telling her again what had happened. It was jumbled, confused, anxious. She sent a message back, 'You lack the season of all natures, sleep.'

I fell into a deep sleep in my leather chair with Spikey on my lap. All would be well. He would comfort me.

JOURNAL

Was the violence of the apprentices a symptom of Elizabethan society or was it something that can happen in any age? As a psychologist, I recognised this type of crowd behaviour, where people lose their individual sense of personal responsibility in a mob and they behave in a way that they would never do if they were alone. We call this 'deindividualization'. An example of this was seen, in the 21st century, with the storming of the Capitol in the USA, when the former president claimed that he had been cheated out of winning the election because the results had been rigged. Four people were killed as a mob forced their way into the building, laughing and joking about what they were doing. A savvy leader knows how to manipulate such behaviour.

CHAPTER 6

T
he day after the incident at The Elephant I ached all over, having slept the night on the chair in the consulting room. I was also confused by what had happened over the last couple of days, culminating in the death of Molly. Indeed, I wasn't sure that I was aware of anything that early in the morning. Was I dreaming? Was I hallucinating? Did I have the plague? I think I may have drifted off to sleep again.

There was a knock at the door, which opened of its own accord. Three women were there, who each greeted me with the salutation, "Hail."

"Hail!" I replied. I looked at them and wondered if they were the three 'witches' who had escaped from the gallows. I couldn't decide. They came in.

One of them said,

"The mind works strangely."

"It plays tricks on you." said a second one, "So that you don't know what is true and what isn't."

"What is real and what isn't," said the third.

"I don't think that it is just the mind that does that." I

retorted. "Politicians play games with us all the time and swear that lies are true!"

"We have a message for you. Listen to what we say. We know where you have come from. You are a ghost from the future."

I told them that I hadn't thought of myself like that. Then the first one stated,

"Beware if reflected fools appear."

The second one added,

"Sleeping brothers are dangerous."

The third one then said,

"Turn three times to ward off foul consequences."

With that, they headed for the door.

"Wait," I said. "You have no control over me and yet you are trying to frighten me. Before you leave, I need to ask you something."

"Ask!" they said in unison. I hesitated because I was somewhat disturbed that I might be getting involved with the occult and falling under their spell. I told myself that such fears were against all my psychological training. Surely these wily actors had been sent by the Globe to test me. This was real theatre and I was in a play without knowing why I was there. But were these the 'escaped witches'?

I asked, "I saw you escape from the gallows. How did you do it?"

They turned the question back.

"How do you think we did it?"

I replied that there was a problem with the two men and the boy being hanged. There was a thunderstorm which led to confusion, followed by their incantations and stamping of their feet.

"Why ask such a question?" demanded the first witch, "If you already know the answer?" Then the second witch started twitching her thumbs between her fingers.

"Macbeth is on his way," she said. "We will leave." Before I could ask again who had sent them, the witches were gone.

There was another knock at the door.

"That'll be Macbeth, Spikey," I said with a laugh. The door opened and I saw a Scotsman standing there, in traditional attire, including a kilt and a knife in his sock.

"Come in!" I told him.

"I will," he said. "My name is… "

"Macbeth!" I answered. "I have been expecting you." He peered at me as if I had said something stupid. After a pause, I said, "I'd been hoping you would come. I presume the theatre has sent you." He laughed and asked if he could sit down. I pointed to the other chair. "You've been here before," I said. "When you were Hamlet."

"Do I look like Hamlet?" He asked. "Am I the same shape, the same age, the same complexion? Do I talk like Hamlet?"

"No, no."

"Well, that is good to know," he replied, asking if now that I had sorted out his identity, that was the end of the first session.

"No of course not." I answered and then I asked, "Why are you here?"

"You want to find out what is on my mind. First, find out what is on your own. Have you met the witches? You see how they operate. Questions are answered with questions or riddles. I answer with the sword and you…? Well, I know your sort, you answer with the pen. Look where it gets you. Christopher Marlowe – dead! Thomas Kyd – dead! You don't learn from others, you scribblers and mind bogglers. I know what I'm doing and what I want."

"And what is that?" I ventured to ask.

"Power – authority, respect and justice."

I replied that it was quite an agenda and I demanded which was the most important.

"All three," he replied.

"But you gave me four!"

"That is what power is about," he snarled. "Justice, respect, authority." He leaned back in his chair.

"And do you not think you have it then?" I asked. He answered that we would have to see. He was to lead the Scots in a defence of their realm by the invading Norwegians on one hand and by a traitorous group of soldiers on the other. His eyes flashed around the room as if he were expecting that we might be interrupted.

"I think I know what you mean," I said. "In my world, the leaders do not fight with the soldiers. They give their orders from many miles away, safe in their well-protected headquarters."

"Not me," he asserted. "I fight for my country. I risk my life in battle and for what? Will I become King as Duncan has promised?

"Duncan has promised?" I questioned.

"He knows that Scotland requires a warrior king and his sons are no warriors. I fight, not from the safety of my castle, but on the battlefield."

I asked if the witches were often with him and he told me that they were. He saw them everywhere, on the battlefields and off them, but they always looked slightly different. He concluded,

"You will not see me for a while." With that, he rose up from the chair and disappeared out of my consulting room.

I sat up and rubbed my eyes. Clearly, my imagination was playing tricks on me. There was no such thing as these witches or Macbeth. They were just a fantasy – a hallucination of a tired mind.

"Was that fantasy or was it a dream?" I asked Spikey, who was now cowering under the cupboard.

JOURNAL

Was I dreaming? As a psychotherapist, I know that anxiety often gives rise to this type of dream and can even cause the dreamer to sleepwalk. What about the prophesies? Do they mean anything? Is my subconscious trying to tell me that in pursuing my quest I might find out secrets that will put me in danger?

Later that day, I received a message from Amelia telling me that a Member of Parliament, Sir Peregrine Stuart Barnes, had requested psychotherapy with the Practice. She assumed that she would be taking on Peregrine as the others in the practice were locums, standing in for Jackie, Ever and me while we were away.

Whilst contacting the practice to make the appointment, Sir Peregrine, or 'Perry' as she called him in private, had been telling Dafydd about his responsibilities in government. Dafydd was surprised to hear him talk of being in government because so far all he knew about him, was that he was a Member of Parliament. If he were a Minister, it was in a very junior role!

CHAPTER 7

O ver the years, the practice *4 Psychotherapists 4 U* has had many well-known clients from the arts, industry, politics, and journalism. Before anyone is accepted as a client, Dafydd, the Practice Manager, conducts a brief investigation into the person concerned, verifying their identity. Then a preliminary session takes place. Each therapist in the practice is supervised by one of their colleagues – as much to ensure the therapist's own well-being as that of the client. Our methodology is for the client to open up the talk at the session. We do not usually ask questions, as to do so might plant ideas into the client's mind, distorting the issues. We simply listen.

Dafydd's initial inquiry into the M.P. had left some questions to be answered, so he decided that he needed to delve further. His investigation revealed that Sir Peregrine Stuart Barnes' birth name was Perry Barnes, but he had changed it to David Osler, then to Barry Fitzwilliam and finally to Peregrine Stuart Barnes. He had been a Member of Parliament for an English constituency on the borders with Scotland, for some years. His party had been in office for most of that period. Background checks showed that he had never made it to the Cabinet. For a very brief time, he had been a junior minister of a 'pop-up' inquiry concerning the importing of valuable tanked tropical fish, possibly illegally. Its emergence followed a furore concerning diseased fish, which had been purchased by parents for their children, and by adults, particularly those over 70. Soon after Christmas, M.P.s were inundated with complaints and certain allegations as to the Prime Minister's involvement in the affair. The Opposition was demanding action. The Prime Minister appointed Peregrine as a Junior Minister, for this one issue only, within the larger Ministry for Agriculture and Fisheries. Perry was, it seems, a pain in the Prime Minister's backside, constantly jockeying for a government position as Perry's wife was the sister of the Party Chairman. To shut him up, the Prime Minister appointed him to be in charge of the Tropical Fish Think Tank, promising awards to come in stages. Firstly, he would be knighted, but 'the greatest was behind,' since later he would be elevated to the House of Lords. All he needed to do was to work on this issue, which would necessitate travelling the world to examine the extent of the problem and then report to the House, exonerating the Prime Minister from any misdoing.

These promises had a profound effect on Perry, who was a short, stocky man. Apparently, he started to 'grow taller' by using heel lifts and elevator shoes. The newspapers had picked up on this, putting it down to him becoming the 'Rising Fishy Minister'. But he was undeterred. He had a group of financial advisers assigned to him and he was to be an international 'statesman'. His advisers, appointed by the PM, decided that he should visit the Cayman Islands, Bermuda, Mauritius, the Bahamas, Panama, Barbados and Guam, while he insisted on going to Iceland, (a place he had always wanted to visit), for a contrast. The list had never been published but one of Dafydd's informants had given it to him noting, that except for Iceland, all the other places were tax havens of some kind. His informant suggested that while Perry was having important discussions with experts on tropical fish, his 'advisers' were having other discussions, checking on a range of unnamed matters. Perry's wife also accompanied him on all these trips, financed privately by her brother.

"My source," Dafydd said with a smile, "seems to imply that the fish tank problem was something of a front." He explained that certain dealings were occurring which were hidden by a 'dead cat' strategy, used to deflect attention from the real purpose of these visits.

When Perry had returned from the investigation he concluded, instructed by the P.M., that all the complaints were false, having been hysterically worked up by a rival tropical fish firm. This was to embarrass the Prime Minister, whose wife, it was reported, had shares in the tropical fish company under investigation. It was acknowledged, that her company had received a lucrative contract from the Government, to supply tropical fish and fish tanks to every one of its departments in Whitehall, to support colleagues, by helping them to work in a serene environment, preventing tensions from boiling over into conflict and mismanagement. Perry also reported that all contracts were above board and no fish were being imported illegally.

"Let me assure the House," Perry had said from the dispatch box, "There was no illegal importing of fish of any kind. It is all a fabrication, promoted by the news media, including the BBC, at the behest of the Opposition." To which there was a loud whisper from the backbench opposite, "What a worthless nerd". At that point the Speaker of the House interrupted, saying that the M.P. had to withdraw the word 'turd' or he would be ejected from the chamber. The M.P. replied,

"I think, Mr. Speaker, that you misheard me refer to the Honourable Member opposite, as a 'turd'. An easy mistake to make, but actually, I said 'nerd' for which I unreservedly apologise." At that, the speaker was overheard asking an attendant, whether the Member said 'turd' or 'nerd?' The attendant shrugged. The debate continued with Perry, waving papers in his hand saying that he could assure members that he had carried out a full internal investigation. Furthermore, he stated, that the Prime Minister had informed the House that an 'inadvertent' mistake had been made regarding him not declaring his wife's shareholdings in this matter.

Perry's day of fame passed without more ado and some weeks later the Prime Minister decided that the role of Junior Minister should be closed. Perry reluctantly had to return to the bank benches, where he sulked.

Later that month, having discussed the matter with the Chairman of the Party, the Prime Minister announced that Perry was to become Sir Peregrine for his services to the country. It was widely rumoured, probably initiated by Perry in the House of Commons tearoom, where he liked to 'hold court', that he would be offered a place in the House of Lords when the Prime Minister produced his next 'honours list'. The Prime Minister must have forgotten this promise because Perry had remained a mere knight on the back benches and had not been elevated. By that time, the initial rumours about the 'fishy affair' and the reason Perry had been given his short-term exposure on the case had died down. He was just Sir Peregrine and apparently, that was that.

Dafydd passed this background to Amelia, who, rolling her eyes, nevertheless agreed to take on the M.P. as a client. There was great anticipation at *4 Psychotherapists 4 U* around Perry's first session with Amelia. Why did he wish to have psychotherapy? They would have to wait and see. Dafydd, however, made it clear that there were to be no 'fishy' references in the Practice relating to the new client that they had 'netted.'

CHAPTER 8

A melia's report to me that a Member of Parliament was to be a new client, brought me back to reality. Having made some notes in my journal, I decided to go for a walk around the neighbourhood, but I was disturbed by the number of crosses that I saw on the doors of people's homes. It was clear that the plague was starting to take hold. When I returned to the consulting room Augustine was waiting for me. "Where have you been?" he asked anxiously.

"Just for a walk to clear my head."

"Are you mad?" he exclaimed. "Didn't you see the crosses on the doors? The theatre has just been closed because of the plague. The company is dividing up and going on tour in the countryside. I'm going with them, but Will Shakespeare has been invited to Wilton House by the Earl of Pembroke. The Earl has invited you as a guest of Will's. Do you want to go?"

"Yes, I'd be delighted but what about my cat?"

"It's a large estate your cat will be fine. I'll go and tell Will." With that Augustine left.

Let me be frank, there was no way that I was going to miss the opportunity of going to Wilton House but also there was no way that I could go there without Spikey. Fortunately, we had, in the consulting room, a rather grand travelling bag that Maddie had made for him when we came here last time. It would neatly fit onto one side of a saddle. l picked up the cat and asked him in a rather childish voice,

"You would like to go to an important Lord's house little one, wouldn't you?" The cat looked at me suspiciously. "Of course, you would," I said, giving him a peck on the nose, which certainly did not please him. He showed his disdain by squirming in my arms until I released him onto the floor, where he went straight back under the cupboard.

Going to Wilton House would be a treat in itself as I would be meeting the Earl of Pembroke, who was the founder of one of the most famous libraries in the world – the Bodleian Library at Oxford. Also, I'd be with Will Shakespeare, but there was something else. The Earl of Pembroke's name was William Herbert and he was a strong candidate for being the Mr W.H. to whom Shakespeare's sonnets were dedicated. I knew that in 1609, 154 of Shakespeare's sonnets, were to be published by Thomas Thorpe. Sonnets are short poems of 14 lines – a format used by many young male poets of the time. Shakespeare started writing the sonnets in the 1590s and the first 126 concerned a relationship with a young man. They were what we would call 'love poems.' So, was the Earl of Pembroke Mr W.H.? No one knows as there were other contenders, such as Henry Wriothesley, (H.W.) the Earl of Southampton, who was still languishing in the Tower of London, because of his involvement in the Essex rebellion. But which of these noblemen, the Earl of Pembroke or the Earl of Southampton, was Mr. W.H.? Shakespeare had dedicated his earlier poems, *Venus and Adonis* and *The Rape of Lucrece* to Henry Wriothesley, so why should he be cryptic about doing so with the Sonnets? Why the initials and not the name? If it were Southampton why not use his full title again and why reverse his initials? If it were William Herbert, the Earl of Pembroke, why not use his title as he had done for Southampton in the earlier poems? And why 'Mr'? It was all rather mysterious and I was determined to find some answers.

This was an opportunity I had not expected. Perhaps while riding I could just ask Will who Mr W.H. was. I thought he might tell me to mind my own business and that would scupper what I was trying to do. On the other hand, if I suggested that it might be Pembroke or Southampton, he might respond with,

"That's interesting. Mr W.H.? I'm not sure either William or Henry would like me to rank them no more than a gentleman. No, I don't know any noblemen who are misters!" I knew that Will was partial to titles and he worked assiduously to gain arms for his family crest. This was going to be a hard nut to crack.

Spikey, Will and I started on our way early in the morning. Luckily our horses were well-behaved. Will was a far more accomplished rider than I imagined. I had never pictured him on a horse before. I realised that I only had a few specific images of him in my mind, which were based on the Gower monument at Stratford, the two famous neo-contemporary likenesses and the bust that overlooks his grave. There are none of him on a horse or showing that he owned one or rode one.

I wondered if Pembroke was journeying to Wilton on horseback or if he was going to use his iron-wheeled coach like the ones that Queen Elizabeth had used. She always travelled with two of them, one to ride in and the other to follow in case there was a problem with the first one. Will told me that Pembroke owned such a coach but that he preferred to travel on horseback, as horses were more comfortable! However, Pembroke was already at his estate and was expecting us later. I have to admit that I was a bit nervous about meeting him. What would he be like?

We rode steadily through the countryside, with overnight staging posts. Heading westward the journey would take three days of good riding with stops at the hostelries along the way. The logistics were part of the job of the lad named Francis, one of the theatre company's employees, who worked out the complex details of the actors' travel arrangements.

At least Spikey seemed happy in his bag, which had been designed so that he could look through netting at the side. Maddie had thought of everything, for which I'm sure Spikey was grateful!

I asked Will about Wilton House and was told that it was an old nunnery, which Pembroke's grandfather had received from a grateful King, Henry Vlll, for his support of the Monarch at the time of the Reformation.

"What is the Earl like? Is he married?" I asked. Will was hesitant.

"No, he isn't married," he told me, "Although in the past, I have told him he should do so."

"Why was that?" I probed, but at that moment, his horse reared up in alarm – possibly from fearing a snake in the grass. The horse and its rider were clearly disturbed.

"Not now, Jacob, not now," he said, "Maybe we can talk about W.H. later. It's complicated."

I changed the subject by asking how the Lord Chamberlain's Men got on when they toured with their plays, whether they walked alongside a horse-drawn cart, like Thespis and his entourage in Ancient Greece. Will told me that some rode and some walked, but if the intended town in which they were to perform was close enough to a port, they would go by boat and then walk. Sometimes they went from one town to another by river and sea, as knowledge of the winds and tides made the journey from say Marlborough to Bristol much faster than it would have been by land. In such circumstances, they would walk south to the channel and get a boat to the Severn estuary and then up to Bristol. If they were going east, say to Norwich, they would go down the Thames and then sail up the east coast. But if they were to perform at Hampton Court, they would just take ferry boats up the river.

Will regaled me with the story of Will Kempe, the 'clown'

who had been with the company for some years until he fell out with them over theatre policy. He then danced to Norwich from London, taking nine days, singing and jesting all the way, criticizing the actors with whom he had worked. According to Will, Kempe thought that he (Kempe) should be the main attraction in a performance. He believed it was he, whom the audiences came to see. He, and another leading actor Richard Burbage, did not get on. The style of the plays was changing, which was leading to much more taxing roles for the comedies. Will felt that these could only be done by Burbage, who was outstanding in them. Kempe believed he was losing credence and took umbrage about Burbage's comic success as Falstaff in *The Merry Wives of Windsor*. Kempe and Burbage argued. Will Shakespeare got well into the story saying, "Kempe then complained to me because I wasn't writing the sort of roles he wanted. His main purpose was to dance complex and comic jigs after the performance. If he did get a role, he would improvise and ruin how the story was progressing. In *Much Ado About Nothing* he claimed that Burbage got a greater laugh from the audience when he tried to sing than he, Kempe, had received throughout the play in the comic role, Dogberry, and for that I was to blame! I eventually told Kempe that if he were unhappy, he should go elsewhere. Kempe was furious and he walked out of the theatre. Unsurprisingly the other actors were not very happy with me or with Burbage and they said that Kempe had been forced out. But we were able to bring in Robert Armin a better comic, who was also a singer. The next I heard of Kempe was that he was dancing his way to Norwich. Kempe had thought that the Lord Chamberlain's Men would go and play there again and that he would be able to return in our boat… but we didn't!"

"Were you upset by all that?" I asked

"Well, of course," he answered. "He was a good comedian and was excellent in *A Midsummer Night's Dream*, but I wanted a different kind of comedian for *Twelfth Night*. I wanted someone with a different kind of voice and humour and with a more subtle style. Robert Armin, who had been working with another theatre group, was perfect for our company. When Kempe stormed out, we approached Armin and he agreed to join us. It made such a difference."

"What happened to Kempe?" I asked.

"He has joined Worcester's Men, but I gather that he is unwell. I was thinking about visiting him. Maybe I will do that when I get back from Wiltshire. I trust he will see me. He just wasn't the man to play Falstaff, that's the pity of it."

Will was an interesting companion and I was looking forward to meeting the mysterious Earl of Pembroke. Would I find out more about their relationship? Tomorrow would tell.

CHAPTER 9

As we approached our destination, I got my first view of Wilton House. The Old Nunnery had been refashioned and was impressive. But it was different from the house I'd once visited in the 21st century. The wonderfully designed Tudor entrance, however, had been built but what I now also saw was the old convent in the process of being developed into a grand Tudor House. It was an imposing building set in wonderful grounds, with expansive access to hunting. I felt a sense of excitement as I entered the gates of the estate but was still rather anxious about meeting Will's 'close friend', with whom I believed there was the possibility that he was in love. Would I find out if he was the 'only begetter' of Will's sonnets?

Will was eager to arrive, as he spurred his horse on to race up the driveway, no doubt to make an impression on the awaiting Earl. The Earl was a handsome, dark-haired young man in his early twenties. He stood, hands on hips, with a broad smile on his face as he watched us from the magnificent entrance to his mansion. He came down and greeted Will with a hug, whilst I deliberately stayed behind. The Earl then came to me and shook my hand warmly before turning back to Will.

Putting his arm around him, he led us past the gate, through the courtyard and towards the Great Hall on the right. I had never been anywhere so impressive. A servant took Spikey in his bag down from the saddle. "Be careful with him," I shouted as the servant walked away, holding the bag containing Spikey at arm's length.

I'm not sure that I made a good impression at my first meeting. I had some nerves of course as Pembroke was one of the most important men in the land. However, he must also have been wary of me, as a man of colour, arriving out of nowhere, who had made friends with a dramatist. Also, the country was experiencing a transition of power from Tudor to Stuart. His Grand House had been given by a Tudor to the Pembrokes, who had thereby benefited from the allegiance to the Tudor Monarchs. Now they would be being watched by Cecil on behalf of the new Stuart King. He would be asking of them and indeed of all the nobles of land, whether they had transferred their loyalty to the new regime. Some, such as Lord Cobham and perhaps Sir Walter Raleigh had not, as the country was about to discover. But what about Pembroke? From his point of view, he must have been wondering about who I was. Will, influenced by Augustine Phillips perhaps, had recommended that I come with him. I was something of an interest, a curiosity, a peculiarity but perhaps he wondered if I were a spy or some other sort of danger.

Pembroke took us into the Great Hall. It was impressive with a large fire burning and a table close to it, where we were to dine. I was pleased to learn that I could stay in the house for some time before I took up lodgings at 'the cottage', somewhere on the estate. We were taken to our rooms by a servant, as we say nowadays, 'to freshen up' after our journey. There were basic facilities supplied, which the servants would empty later.

As I came down, I saw one of the servants whispering something to the Earl, who looked puzzled. Will hadn't yet joined us.

"Come and sit with me. Jacob, isn't it? Have some refreshments." I was given a mug of excellent cider. "Made with our own apples you know," Pembroke said, "The finest in the land, fit for the King if he were to come and visit." I raised my eyebrows in surprise and laughed nervously. "I gather from Joseph here," he nodded towards the servant, "That you have a cat with you."

"Yes Sir," I said, not knowing the protocol about how to address him.

"Sir? You don't have to call me 'Sir' you can call me Pembroke or W.H., which is how I am known to my friends." I wondered if I'd solved the age-old problem of Mr W.H. but I returned to the subject of the cat.

"Yes W.H.," I said, "His name is Spikey and he goes everywhere with me," I added quickly that he had a flea collar which prevented him from catching fleas. He looked surprised.

"How do they work?" he asked. I explained that they have a toxin within them and that it is released gradually and spreads over the body of the cat, killing the fleas.

"And what happens if the toxins, as you call them, which sound like poisons, run out?"

"I fit a new collar," I said.

He laughed and commented, "They told me at the theatre that you were a strange one but be careful with domesticated cats. In this country, they are often associated with witches and I must tell you, so are black people." He paused and I nodded my understanding. He smiled and continued, "Spikey may stay in your room with you." He then nodded to Joseph, who went to leave us. "And Joseph," he said, "Make sure that Spikey is well fed."

Will came and joined us as we sat down for an afternoon dinner, which was a venison casserole with plenty of fresh, warm and crusty bread as well as more cider.

After dinner, we smoked plentiful pipes provided for us by W.H. My suspicions of the intimacy between him and Will were gaining credence. I admit I liked him. He had a certain charm, a wicked smile and a sparkle in his eyes. He clearly liked the company of men. There were no women around when I arrived, although the ones who appeared later in my stay, were all vivacious.

He was a man who loved his comforts. His home had sumptuous soft furnishings and exquisite medieval murals on morally religious themes that were to be found in various rooms. None of them had been whitewashed out, despite the orders of Henry Vlll and Edward Vl. W.H. and his father had more or less ignored such laws but some of the 'extreme' Roman Catholic art, I was told, had been covered over to avoid destruction. These precious items were far too good to obliterate, whatever the religious persuasion of the Monarch. I suspected that W.H. didn't adhere to any form of religion, although publicly he behaved as expected and went to the Established State Church regularly. But why not? It wouldn't have been politically sound to do otherwise. Why give up the pleasures of life for religion – whichever side of the religious divide you might find yourself on? Better to be pragmatic and go with the flow – or rather with what the King wants!

The hospitality that night and throughout my stay was overwhelming. W.H. loved his food, wine and smokes. He was a liberated man, who was able to indulge in his passions owing to his wealth and generosity towards others. Although political, he did not seem to be a man to bear a grudge or delightfully indulge in the misfortune of others.

So, we spent the evening smoking his pipes and drinking wine whilst conversing about the theatre. Will mentioned to W.H. that the company was considering putting on a new play *The Tragedy of Gowrie*, which was about the attempted kidnapping in Scotland of the King by the Gowrie brothers, and the Scottish King's 'brave' fight with the kidnappers, who were killed in the skirmish by the King's guards.

W.H. shook his head at the thought of such a play and said that it would be dangerous.

"You don't think that was what happened do you?" he asked.

"Well, there is a pamphlet that has reported it," said Will.

W.H. questioned, "But Will, with whom did the pamphlet originate? Think about it. The King owed £80,000 to John Ruthven, the Earl of Gowrie's father. The King had Ruthven arrested and executed for treason, so he thought the debt might be cancelled. However, Gowrie's sons still demanded repayment of the full amount. The King's story, as reported in that pamphlet, was that he was kidnapped and taken to the Gowrie estate. There he was led up to the top room of a tower, where he fought off his kidnappers. The King's men saw him there (how would they know where to look?) and came up to rescue him. There is also the question of how the guards would have had time to get from the ground, up to the top of the tower. They killed the Gowrie brothers in the fight that followed. The King let it be known that he fought bravely and overcame his kidnappers, enhancing his reputation as a skilful fighter. But isn't it possible that he had his soldiers in position to burst in and kill the Gowrie brothers? It could have been the King who set the trap! Which version do you think is likely to be closer to the truth, the King was tricked and taken to the estate, or that he went to the estate with his men expressly to kill the brothers and put an end to his debt?"

"Of course, the victor always puts his version forward as the truth. The play was showing the version that the King had given us and therefore there is no reason to ban it!" Will said defensively.

"That may be all well and good, but the Scottish Kirk didn't believe him! If the play were put on, the whole issue would be raised again. You don't use stories about the Monarch and you certainly don't put his personal history on the stage." I could see that W.H. showed political acumen. W.H. went on to tell Will to have nothing to do with the play about Gowrie. After all, the King was planning to change the name of the theatre company from The Chamberlain's Men to The King's Men. Being connected with a play about the King would be political suicide, whatever the truth of the actual event might be.

Will went deep into thought. After a while he said,

"I am already working on an alternative play, set in Vienna about a Duke rather than a King."

"And are you intending to criticise the Duke?" probed W.H. "Or to criticise him, while overtly seeming to pander to his vanity?"

"I'll be measured in what I say. One measure against another measure! All taking place far from London, England or Scotland." W.H. nodded his approval but added,

"'Measure for Measure' is a biblical quote and you need to be careful with religious issues. The new King is not going to prove as lenient as people might think either to the Catholics or to the Puritanical Brownists."

Perhaps this was giving me an insight into the true religious leanings of Will and his friends. They lived in a world of Christian turmoil but at least they were wise enough to keep themselves clear of controversy. Writing something well-measured was what was needed and which would prove acceptable to the authorities and to the audience.

Throughout this banter, I kept quiet. Then I bid the others goodnight and went to my room, leaving Will and W.H. together, chatting amicably. It was apparent to me, that W.H. was a significant donor and supporter of the theatre in more ways than one.

I thought that Spikey must be wondering where I was and I had some nice scraps for him from the afternoon's meal. I realised that he was happy enough when, as I entered the room, he presented me with a mouse that he had caught and half devoured. I also noticed that he had been given food by one of the servants. Nevertheless, he still enjoyed my scraps during the night.

As I lay in bed, I wondered if Mr W.H. was William Herbert and if Will was in love with him. I was living in the same house. Surely, I could find out – maybe this very night W.H. and Will could be sleeping together. Christianity fostered guilt and then punished it. Yet love between a man and a woman, a man and a man, a woman and a woman surely, surpasses prejudice in the eyes of love itself. How in the morning would they feel? According to Sonnet 35,

> No more be grieved at that which thou hast
> done:
> Roses have thorns and silver fountains mud.
> Clouds and eclipses stain both moon and sun,
> And loathsome canker lives in sweetest bud.

I wondered about the relationship, not for some puerile reason but rather to solve a mystery of over 400 years. I hoped indeed that they were in love if that could bring happiness. But I also wondered if the poet could simultaneously be in love with his wife. Why not? Many have loved both men and women. Does love negate itself by being deceitful? Isn't it deceit and not love, that is the fault, if all partners are content with what is and what is not? I prefer not to judge. I analyse and thereby try to help, even when the world appears to condemn. I heard W.H. and Will coming up to bed. Was it one door that closed or was it two? Furthermore, what did it matter? I realised that I did not need to find out. Let people be!

JOURNAL

This is going to be more of an adventure than I had imagined. Pembroke hinted that the King might even stay at the house later in the year. There would be no way I would be presented to him, but I trusted that at least I might get sight of him and hear gossip about what was being said. I needed to keep my ear to the ground. Maybe the servants might talk or the actors when, and if they came. Gossip and rumour are interesting but usually include a lot of half-truths and speculation. I am fully aware of the influence of fake news in my own time. Look at how civilians and the press posted photo after photo of the war in Ukraine, which Russia claimed were 'staged', stating that the Ukrainians were bombing their own people. Two completely different accounts of the same event. How would these events be recorded in the future? Which narrative would gain dominance and be remembered in history? Almost certainly the version belonging to the victor! Recording history is not about recording the truth, but about political expediency and what the dominant group wants to be portrayed. Belief is important in this process. Most people believe what they are told to believe – whether Jew, Muslim, Hindu, Buddhist, Christian, Protestant, Puritan or Catholic. Whatever powerful force is in control, whether in a dictatorship or a democracy, it attempts to impose its ideology on the people. It was ever thus!

CHAPTER 10

I had a restless night with issues on my mind, haunting me. I was still thinking about Will and W.H. Despite my moral reservations, before falling asleep, I wondered, in the morning, if I should wait until I knew everyone had left the bedrooms and then 'peep' into them to see if they'd been used – or at least if Shakespeare's had been left vacant. Yet what courtesy would that be? I tried to put it from my mind, thinking of Hamlet.

'Why, look you now, how unworthy a thing you make of me!
You would play upon me; you would seem to know my stops,
you would pluck out the heart of my mystery...'

I drifted into a shallow sleep and heard voices. I walked across to the window, where people were talking near the great doors below me. I looked out and could hardly believe what I saw. In the moonlight there was a man in conversation with W.H. He looked a little like the Scot who had visited me in London and whom I had presumed to be Macbeth, but no, it wasn't him. I couldn't hear what they were saying but I watched as they shook hands. He then mounted his horse and rode away, while W.H. returned to the house. Was this yet another dream? Had I sleep-walked to the window?

The next morning, I thought I needed to take stock. W.H. in advising against the Gowrie play, could mean that Will might consider another Scottish theme. Writers use their environment as inspiration, so I wanted to find out more about the house where Will sometimes stayed. I decided to look around.

I examined the sculptures in the Great Hall, many of which had religious connotations. One showed a man wounded by arrows, but there was no inscription to show if it was St Sebastian or some other soldier, who had been used as target practice. That was part of the reformation problem. Certain people were hanging on to the 'Old Faith' but the dilemma was that this 'Old Faith' was connected to the Pope in Rome, who exercised not just religious but political influence. The Popes were as much political manipulators and imperialists as any of the Kings in Europe. The rituals of the church were such that they sacramentally gave power to Kings, bishops and priests, which they believed came from God. To me, it all seemed nonsense, but it was embedded in the fabric of society. Henry Vlll had held onto Catholicism but of his own Anglican variety, merging it with his sense of responsibility to rule, since he believed that his authority came from God. All the Tudors, including 'Bloody Mary' who executed Protestants, believed that they were divinely appointed. Elizabeth tried for a 'via media' but the Pope excommunicated her, which gave anyone 'saintly' and brave enough, a licence to try and murder her. No wonder she, or at least the Cecils on her behalf, started to execute the English so-called missionary priests. These were priests who were trained aboard and had come back to England to reconvert the people.

Next, I walked over to the old convent chapel, which was still intact, with a fresco of a crucifixion on the wall above the altar. It was an extraordinary example of medieval art, although there were cracks across it and it was certainly showing its age. The flaking image of Christ was one on which he hung on the cross, with his head erect and his eyes looking straight ahead of him. There was no realism here. It was an icon of the late medieval church. Beneath the Christ figure were two women looking up towards him and a man, looking outward towards infinity. The man's hand was pointing upwards, towards the figure of Christ on the cross. Christ's arms, outstretched, were encompassing the world as if with love. It was quite remarkable. It was not Christ in agony but Christ in love with whoever was looking at the painting.

"You like the fresco?" a voice came from behind me. I turned and saw W.H. who had slipped into the chapel without me hearing him. There were no chairs or pews in the room and he was just standing at the back of this ornate place of worship.

"Yes, I do," I replied. "I hope it will survive the test of time."

"By law, it should have been whitewashed out, together with the images of the apostles on the sides of the chapel," he said, pointing to one of them. "This is our Judas Iscariot. Look, it is fading but he appears to be holding the rope with which he will hang himself. He was not truthful to his friends you know!"

He gave me a piercing stare which made me feel uneasy. I hadn't noticed the particularities of the other frescoes, in my concentration on the central one, but it was true. Iscariot the traitor, whom we are told betrayed his Lord with a kiss, was there holding the instrument of his eventual suicide. But was he a 'traitor', doing it for the money? Perhaps he 'betrayed' with good intent, to galvanise Christ into political action. If so, maybe he just didn't understand Christ's mission at the time and later realised he had made a huge mistake!

I thought back to my knowledge of Shakespeare's *Macbeth*.

"What do you believe a traitor is?" I asked W.H. He

laughed and said he'd asked Will that very same question and Will had replied, "One that swears and lies. They swear loyalty to the King and yet lie about it. Beneath the swearing, they know that in their minds they are thinking something different, which is hidden by the words used."

"Equivocation you mean?" I asked. "But what if it is the King who swears and lies?"

W.H. leaned closer to me and said, "I don't think such things. To do so is to question the King's authority and that would undermine the oath that I have sworn." I told him that I understood but pressed him a little further saying,

"I was just interested in what happens if someone swears a loyalty to the King but also to a religious leader, such as the Pope." He smiled and said it could cause chaos if the two leaders disagreed. That is why Henry Vlll had taken charge of the church. He thought it would prevent the temptation to be equivocal if someone swore an oath one way, but in their mind, they believed the opposite.

"A recipe for disaster," I said, to which he responded,

"One can't control people's minds, but I gather you are a mind doctor so you must know about that." I replied that he was right about my profession and that the mind was often pulled in two directions. However, this in itself leads to tension.

"Do you, as a doctor, correct that?" he asked.

"That's not my purpose." I said, "I listen and allow the person to articulate their dilemmas and come to their own answers, finding their own solution by talking to me."

"So, the important thing for you is to listen?"

"Yes," I replied, "Also to watch as this can give me an indication as to the veracity of what is being said or not said. But I am not like a spy, just an observer of human behaviour." He told me that he realised now, why Augustine and Will were interested in me.

"It is obvious," he said, "That religion and politics are

mixed, but maybe the Protestant faith was the one that had brought England its freedom from Rome. It allowed it to break free and find its own culture to govern itself independently in trade and the development of literature and the arts. After all, my uncle was Sir Philip Sydney the great poet warrior of Elizabeth's reign, inspiring artistic development."

W.H. was proud of his heritage but also of his learning. He showed me his extensive library and said that I could use it as I wished and although I was going to live in the cottage, I could have books sent to me. He left me in the library to read. I found Holinshed's *Chronicles of England Scotland and Ireland* and I sat down to read more about the historical figure of Macbeth King of Scotland, who reigned in the 11th century.

On my return to my room from the library, I picked up Spikey. He had been much friendlier towards me as if he were keeping an eye on me. Also, he seemed pleased with the higher class of food that he was being served.

"What do you think of this place Spikey?" I asked but he looked at me as if to say, 'That's enough attention for now.' He started to struggle so I put him down. He went to the corner of the room where the servants had put a cushion for him, which he had happily made his own.

JOURNAL

To have been speaking with the nephew of Sir Philip Sydney must be one of the most fascinating experiences of my life. He gave me the impression of an encyclopaedic culture of learning found within his family and following his earlier advice to me to take care, he never once commented on my skin colour. He was a Lord and I was a commoner but he treated me with great courtesy and interest. I felt at times that our minds met.

We had talked about equivocation that night. I think our 21st century politicians do it all the time. If asked, 'Did you attend parties during lockdown?' The response was that there were business meetings at which there were refreshments. Under further questioning the politicians said that there were 'gatherings' at which alcohol and food were served. But these were not 'parties'. It was an example of 21st century equivocation, a political discourse involving deliberate obfuscation and a dishonest use of language.

CHAPTER 11

Perry arrived late for his first appointment with Amelia. When he finally walked in, Dafydd asked him for his name. The M.P. looked at him condescendingly and said,

"Don't you know who I am?"

Dafydd looked at his computer and thought to himself, "Well, you could be Perry Barnes, David Osler, Barry Fitzwilliam or Peregrine Stuart Barnes, but to his face, Dafydd said,

"Are you Mr Stuart Barnes?"

"Sir Peregrine Stuart Barnes," he corrected him.

"You must be here to see Dr Fortune but the appointment should have started half an hour ago."

"Important matters – delayed," replied Peregrine pompously.

"I will see if Dr Fortune can fit you in now."

Having phoned Amelia's office, he showed Perry into her room.

"Oh, Dr Fortune, you are female," said Perry, frowning.

"Is that a problem?"

"No, I suppose not. But I was expecting someone called Jacob."

"That is my husband, Dr Fortune, but he is away at the moment. Do you wish to continue with me?"

"Well, I suppose you will have to do, as long as you are qualified."

"I can assure you that I am. Please take a seat." Amelia smiled, whilst indicating the chair.

In therapy sessions, it is not merely what is said which is important. Amelia noted that Perry was quite small in stature, despite his raised shoes, but interestingly, his clothes seemed to be rather big on him. She put these thoughts to one side and said, "I understand that our Practice Manager has already sent you some information and that he has explained the nature of the psychotherapeutic process to you. During the time you are in the consulting room, you can talk in complete confidence about whatever is concerning you. My role is to listen."

Perry sat down with some unease. This was not like the tea room in the House of Commons, in fact, it was a very different cup of tea. He took out a piece of paper and saying that he understood that he had to start the session, began to read,

"I am Sir Peregrine Stuart Barnes, one-time Minister of Fisheries and now a backbencher. You may call me Sir Peregrine. After all, my name is my identity and my knighthood is my status in society. You will have realised that I am a descendent of the Royal Stuarts. I work in London and my wife Camilla and I spend my holidays in Scotland at Balmoral, in a cottage that I rent annually from the Monarch, to whom I have had the honour to be presented on four occasions. It should have been five but sadly I fractured my foot on the day that I was to drive to Windsor and I ended up in hospital." (Dafydd had mentioned earlier to Amelia that Perry had actually run over his own foot by getting out of the car without engaging the brake). Perry stopped reading.

"That's all you need to know about me. Was that what you

were looking for?" Perry condescendingly asked Amelia. She reminded him that he still had some consultation time left.

"You can tell me whatever you want, for example, why are you here?" Then she sat silently. When she didn't continue, he said irritably, "Well, is it or isn't it? Should I go or should I stay?" Amelia remained silent. "Are you psychoanalysing me?" he asked aggressively, "Because if you are, you should tell me what you are thinking." Amelia still remained silent. "Well, I'll tell you what you are thinking," he said. "You are thinking why is such an important man, a descendant of the Stuarts, with many years of experience in the House of Commons, and who has been presented privately to the Monarch on four separate occasions, coming to you for psychotherapy? Well, if you want an answer, I'll tell you." He seemed anxious and a little hostile. He paused and then went on rather angrily, "I believe I've been cursed by a witch. My life has been ruined by something evil." He suddenly put his head in his hands and when he looked up again Amelia, for a moment, saw a distraught man beneath the façade which he had shown up until then. Maybe he had broken through a barrier?

"Cursed?" she asked.

"So, you do speak!" Perry stated sarcastically. As his façade re-emerged he went on the defensive, "This is a game that you cleverly use to humiliate your clients is it not?" Perry was obviously frightened and he was quiet for some minutes. Amelia waited. Eventually, he sighed heavily and began to tell his story.

"We nearly lost the last election, or rather my colleagues did because as usual, I held on to my seat comfortably. My constituents are loyal and grateful for my care and attention. In returning to power with a reduced majority the Prime Minister, on the occasion of the Monarch's official birthday, decided to reward some of the losers in the election, who had served him, promoting them to the House of Lords. He had promised to do this for me," he paused and then said angrily, "But he didn't. He sat in number ten and produced a list of honours for those who had failed, but I, who had succeeded, was nowhere to be seen. It was unfair. Basil Thornton, who lost his seat, was elevated into the Peerage but I, who had given my all, was neglected. What had Basil Thornton ever done? Ever heard of him? Of course, you haven't. He's done nothing but I saved the P.M., Bertram Farquhar's political life in the famous fish debate in the Commons. I triumphed over our foes, but he didn't even give me a job in the Cabinet. Instead, he returned me to the back benches in the House of Commons with nothing but my knighthood. If it hadn't been for me, there would have been a scandal that would have embarrassed him for the rest of his life.

Then, when I was working in the Bahamas, one of my advisers, whom I'd entertained for drinks, informed me that our P.M. was having an extramarital relationship with Helena Rousseau, that is *the* Helena Rousseau, the television journalist. Would you believe it? Not even social media had picked up on it. Helena Rousseau, the scourge of politicians! It was now being rumoured that Farquhar was considering appointing her to the House of Lords. I was having none of that, I had brought down bigger men than him, former Ministers and Leaders of our Party. Even members of the Royal Family have been humiliated and their reputations destroyed by me, far more than by Helena Rousseau. I decided that the Prime Minister had to go. I started to investigate in places where only I knew where to investigate. I knew his sordid little background."

Amelia noted that he had fallen into a state of excited self-satisfaction at what he was telling her.

"Knowledge is power," he said nodding at her, and then stared into the distance behind her. "I wrote to him at his private home, mentioning Rousseau. I told him that he was a coward and a traitor to his wife, family and the party. I posted the letter marked 'personal', saying that I would tell all if I didn't get my promised place in the House of Lords." He looked at Amelia to ensure that she was still engaged in his revelation. She nodded while thinking how stupid the man was to put anything in writing.

Perry leaned back in his chair and laughed. He continued, "I could have destroyed him if I had leaked it to the press. He was the man who promoted himself as a guardian of family values. If Helena Rousseau was going to the House of Lords, so was I!" He paused for a moment and blinked profusely. He seemed on the verge of tears. Repositioning himself on his seat, he continued, "How could I have known when he read the letter, that he had a bad heart?" Perry's demeanour now changed again as he repeated "How could I know that? I couldn't have been expected to know that his heart was weak and the stress of his post as P.M. was too great. But just after he had read the letter, he had a heart attack and died in his living room, with my letter still in his hand: in the living room – dead! I couldn't have ever dreamt that such a thing would happen. It was not my intention. It was a lamentable accident, caused by his inability to do his job and unfortunate timing." Perry now composed himself, as he continued, "At the funeral, which was a grand affair, I was able to sit just seven rows from the front, walking down the aisle, nodding my greetings to everyone, including the Prince of Wales. I had met him at the door and he walked down the aisle after me!

Later that week, I went to the late P.M.'s widow's private home to express my condolences. However, the widow alleged that I was the one who had triggered her husband's death. She told me that her husband had died as a result of my threats and the blackmail contained within a letter which she had taken from her husband's hand before the medics arrived. She then told me that she had powers beyond mine. She showed me to the door and said that she had 'cursed me', in the name of her husband. 'Farquhar's curse!' she said, would follow me wherever I went for the rest of my life. I thought that it was all rubbish. But immediately strange things started to happen to me."

Amelia waited for him to explain, as his demeanour changed yet again.

"Mrs Farquhar had hardly finished telling me that I had been cursed when, as I got to the front door, I tripped over this cursing woman's black cat. I fell against a table, knocking down a mirror from the wall. The glass shattered. Mrs Farquhar, like a witch, laughed and screeched 'black cats and mirrors'." After a few seconds to check that Amelia was still listening, he continued, "It was raining outside as she pushed me out, saying what a naughty cat she had, to trip up such a 'good man' and cause the mirror to crash all around him. But there was more to come. There was a flash of lightning followed by a thunderclap. I got soaking wet as I made for my car. I was distracted because the feelings from this incident stayed with me. On my way home, another cat ran in front of me and in trying to avoid it I drove my car into some water. A police car happened to be behind me. When they saw what had happened, they breathalysed me and although I was below the limit, the press got hold of the story and I was being ridiculed as 'the wet fish M.P. who drove into the sea'. Apparently, *Private Eye* has a photo and are intending to put me on their front page."

Perry paused, shuddered and continued, "Yesterday the tax office asked to see me about my travel expenses, which I incurred when I was Minister of Fisheries. The press are now suggesting that I exaggerated my expenses and questioned my need for foreign travel, particularly my need to go to Iceland. They just don't understand the nature of the investigation, but they are implying other issues relating to the trip. Yet I am in the clear. I had no secret handouts, no dealings with Russian or Chinese agents, no hedge fund speculations nor insider dealings and perhaps therefore I am not cursed. Perhaps this is all in my mind, owing to the stress I am under, hearing about the death of a colleague. That's it. That is the cause of my condition. I am in grief." He stood up making himself as tall as possible and strode towards the door.

Amelia told him that she would be happy to see him again. He replied that he would consider the offer and perhaps might return but it would probably not be necessary. As he left, he said to her, "You know I could have talked to myself in a mirror and said everything that I have told you today. I would have saved myself a lot of money!"

Amelia sent me her report, saying that she felt she needed to be careful as Perry was a self-obsessed and spiteful man, in whom the press were currently taking an interest. I agreed that he could be dangerous and that she should report to me after their next meeting. There could be a further significant scandal over the tropical fish affair but as a practice, we would need to abide by client confidentiality. Only in that respect are we like priests in a confessional box.

CHAPTER 12

I t was through Amelia that I heard that Jackie, still
disguised as me, and Ever were doing well in Oxford.
They had taken long stay accommodation with the
Davenants at the Salutation Tavern. Jackie, as Dr Jacob
Fortune, had opened a discreet 'MIND' clinic in one of the
tavern's rooms. Her clients were mainly students. She helped
them, with what we think of as depression. In the seventeenth
century, people considered that the cause of this malady was
physical, brought about by an imbalance of the 4 bodily
humours: blood, yellow bile, black bile, and phlegm. A surfeit
of any of them would lead to a different outcome. It was a
superfluity of black bile, for example, which resulted in
melancholy. Although we knew otherwise, neither Jackie in
Oxford, nor I in London contradicted the science of the time.
We just used our skills to listen and support our clients, using
the vocabulary with which they themselves were familiar. Jackie
did wonder whether some people came to her because she was
of colour and that maybe she had magical powers. She didn't
profess to have these but used her communication skills and
understanding of human behaviour to help her clients.

A back room was emptied by Jane Davenant, usually known

as Jennet, which allowed Ever to set up business as a seamstress, specialising in clothes that students could purchase for their girlfriends. Women of course were not allowed to be members of the University. Undergarments were produced for young women but also some married ones wishing to give their men a thrill. It was all quite bizarre and maybe 400 years before its time. She made a few garments for the male students to wear beneath their compulsory styles of dress. On the quiet, she could wrestle up any garment desired, including bogus Oxford gowns or religious vestments, particularly of the old church and only for use in private, of course. A Roman Mass was illegal and the authorities were always on the lookout for Jesuit priests arriving to minister to the recusants. But Ever was happy to undertake any orders. No questions asked because frankly, she didn't think it was a problem. Neither of the women advertised but they got sufficient business by word of mouth.

Cecil's spies, of course, knew much of what was going on regarding recusant Catholics, but it was more advantageous for them to listen and watch rather than blow their cover.

However, this trade in church vestments worried Amelia, as Jackie and Ever could be discovered not as money makers but as sympathetic recusants.

"You are playing with fire," Amelia told them when she found out what Ever was doing. "You could be in great trouble if you provide these garments to Catholic priests!" She then went on to raise another point, that during psychotherapy students could reveal things about themselves that could place Jackie in significant trouble in the church courts, if not the civil ones. In London, they'd had a regular clientele from the theatre and from the government itself, some of whom, of course, could have been spies. But in Oxford, the range of clientele was different. Amelia advised them to move out of the city as soon as possible.

It was at this time that they recognised one of the guests at the Tavern, who seemed to be a great friend of the Davenants, and particularly of Jennet. She told them that the man often stayed there on his way to Stratford, where his wife and family lived. "Sometimes," Jennet added, "He just comes here to get out of London and clear his head from his scribbling." She laughed, "But he's always scribbling. He often stays with us in the spring. Look, here he is now."

They looked up and saw Will walk into the public room where they were sitting. They recognised him from the Globe. He came up to Jennet and greeted her warmly. She then went to serve other customers in another area. Jackie felt the game must be up. She knew that Will had been with me at Wilton, but he showed no surprise at seeing her. He started chatting to her as if she were me. Will was particularly interested in the therapy that Jackie was offering for students with 'problems of the mind'. They also talked about London and the fact that the Davenants had lived close to the theatre and had been good friends with him. He told them about his home in Stratford, with his wife Anne and his daughters Susanna and Judith and the fact that his son Hamnet had died. They deduced that he had experienced quite enough of death as within a short space of time his mentor and friend James Burbage had died and also his father, whom he greatly missed. They felt sorry for him and without thinking, Jackie placed her hand in his in comfort and understanding.

"You are kind," he whispered, looking at her hand. "Let me reciprocate your kindness. You, Jacob, cannot be here and also at Wilton, where I know you are, because I have recently left there. This small hand betrays your femininity. One day it could get you into trouble."

Jackie and Ever were immediately concerned at the discovery and asked if Jennet knew. Will said, "Of course, Jennet has washed clothes for you." He smiled and added that in his plays he had often dealt with the issue of cross-dressing. Jackie and Ever had been rumbled by an actor and an innkeeper, but it would be more serious if their secret had been discovered by one of Cecil's spies. Will advised them to leave Oxford as soon as possible. They could go to Stratford. His wife took in lodgers and could find work for them. They should be safer there. Jackie and Ever considered this and decided to leave as soon as they were able to make appropriate arrangements.

Later that day Jennet reinforced Will's sound advice. As strangers in Oxford, Jackie and Ever might be under suspicion and were probably already being watched. Will's suggestion, that they should go to stay with his wife Anne in Stratford, was a good one. She had some rooms to let and possibly some work for them. Ever should not deliver any of the clothes she was working on, to any client and certainly, she should get rid of the church vestments. Indeed, if she left them in a safe place, Jennet would be able to dispose of them.

"We will get you out of here as soon as possible," said Jennet. "Go to Shipston-on-Stour, dressed as Jacob and Ever, to lodgings that I know. Stay the night and then depart in the morning as Jackie and Ever, sisters-in-law on their way to meet friends and relatives in Stratford. If you can avoid it, do not speak to anyone here in the tavern and certainly not that man over there drinking by the window.

"Why not him?" Ever asked in alarm.

"Have you met him before?" Jennet asked.

"Only briefly. He saw me yesterday in town and said he may have some work for me."

"He is the reason why you need to move fast," Jennet said. "His name is Nicholas Owen although he is registered here under a different name. She then whispered, "He is a Jesuit – keep clear. It can be dangerous to be associated with Roman Catholics!"

Jackie and Ever decided to go to their room whilst Jennet went across and had a word or two with the man at the window, who then immediately left the premises.

JOURNAL

I wondered about the Jesuits and what they were doing there. It was a religious order founded by a former soldier in Spain, to ensure that people lived the life of the Church and so in death came to God. They were Roman Catholic and many were ardent young English men trained abroad in the wake of the accession to the throne of the 'Protestant' Queen Elizabeth. Some then returned to England to try and restore the Old Faith, even if that meant trying to assassinate the Monarch. If apprehended they were horribly executed. I considered that they had been brainwashed into fanaticism, which they thought would lead to martyrdom. I can't help thinking about similarities with other young religious fanatics, of various faiths, in the 21st century.

CHAPTER 13

Back at Wilton House, I realised again that the mind plays tricks on me as well as on my clients, but I was finding difficulty in distinguishing between the various realities in which I was engaging. I kept seeing that Scotsman. Was he real or was he an illusion? Was he spying on me? At least the witches had not appeared again.

Will had gone off to Oxford and I later learned that W.H. had been called back to London. He said that someone would look after me but except for the servants ensuring that I was fed, there didn't appear to be anyone else taking an interest in me, unless it was the Scotsman, if he existed. I asked one of the servants, Adam, about him and he mimicked the Scottish accent saying, "You'll find nae Scotch here unless it be under the bed." I didn't know what he meant but later I was so troubled that I looked under the bed and scolded myself for being so stupid.

We did however have some visitors. I heard a commotion early one afternoon and saw from the library window that some actors had arrived. They were coming up the drive with two carts filled with stage props. Augustine was riding a horse and was accompanied by a diminutive actor, although clearly an important one, for he too was also on a horse. They didn't come to the main house but went round the side towards the stables and outhouses. They had their lodgings in a large barn which was also where they would be able to rehearse.

Augustine came to see me later that afternoon. After the usual courtesies, the two of us had dinner together, during the course of which he asked me how things were going with the house. He wondered whether I found anything strange about it. At first, I replied that I hadn't but then I came clean about my anxieties. I told him that I kept seeing a Scotsman and indeed I thought that I had once met him soon after I had arrived in London. He listened intently and said to me,

"Don't you realise Jacob, that you are like a ghost to us? You have come from another place, just like a ghost." I felt a chill in my spine and clearly lost colour in my face. Augustine laughed. "Maybe you are consulting with us as a ghost Jacob." I protested that the Scotsman seemed so real. Augustine simply replied, "As you do to us and we do to you." He looked at me intently before continuing. "The new King is superstitious, especially about ghosts, witches, black people and the supernatural, which could cause you a problem."

He continued by telling me a story about events related to the marriage of the Scottish King and his Queen. "There had been a diplomatic arrangement for the Scottish King to marry the Princess of Denmark and she was supposed to come to Scotland for the wedding. She attempted to do so but there were huge storms resulting in her ship having to take shelter in Norway. She tried several times to sail to Scotland but the storms were too great. Someone in Norway suggested that it was because of the Scottish witches. Therefore, the King decided that he would brave the storms and go to her in Norway. This he did and he married her there before they went on to Copenhagen to celebrate the marriage. When they tried to return to Scotland their journey was again delayed by terrible storms and once again, some said that it was the result of witchcraft.

When the King and Queen eventually got back to Scotland, over 100 'witches' were rounded up. He actively interrogated some himself, including one named Agnes Sampson, who at first denied any involvement. They searched her for the Devil's Mark on her body, stripping her naked and torturing her. They even forced a witch's bridle into her mouth and had her stretched up against the wall with her hands held high and her feet only just touching the floor, totally exposing her to her torturers. Not surprisingly, she eventually 'confessed' and named other so-called 'witches'. There followed mass burnings of a large number of women in Scotland who were judged to be of the 'devil's clan', as are black men, or even half-black people such as you, Jacob. The King was having his revenge for the storms that had disrupted their journeys, which he believed were instigated by witches. This was the man who was now ruling England!"

We talked about this for a while but after Augustine had left, I seriously thought whether I should continue with my mission. However, to change anything would have been a failure. I felt that I needed to contact Amelia. I sent a note to her.

My Dearest Amelia.

The new regime here is wrought with superstitions, discrimination and false conclusions. My work as a psychotherapist may be just too soon. Despite the wisdom we find in the plays by Will, I doubt if I can 'raze out the written troubles of the brain' in this barbarous age.

Love Jacob

I received a stern reply from Amelia.

Dear Jacob

"Barbarous age! Don't you think it compares to the

barbarity of our times or that of our fathers and
grandfathers, by the political elite – for example, the needless
slaughter of English and German soldiers on Flanders fields,
Hitler's Holocaust, the systematic bombing of Dresden, the
dropping of the atomic bomb on the cities Hiroshima and
Nagasaki, the use of napalm taking the skin off people in
Vietnam, the mass murders in Cambodia, the invasion of
Iraq, the invasion of Ukraine, the conflicts over the Middle
East with atrocities in Israel and Gaza. Come off it, Jacob,
humans are barbarous animals. To counter that at least we
have the creativity in the arts, music, poetry and the wonders
of theatre. Keep to your task, find out more about that
incredible play *Macbeth*, which predates by four centuries the
work of Freud."

Love,

Amelia

I had clearly hit a raw nerve with my wife, but she was
correct. I needed to stop whining and get on with the project in
hand.

There was a knock at the door as I was dozing off. I swiftly
picked up a book.

"Come in!" I called. Adam entered and gave me a letter
from W.H. It said that the King was again considering coming
to Wilton house. I would have to move into the cottage and I
was to warn Augustine and the servants that all should be made
ready. Augustine should prepare something for the King's
entertainment. There was a postscript saying that the King
disapproved of tobacco and that I was to tell Adam to hide all
of W.H.'s pipes.

I immediately discussed the matter of the King's
unexpected visit with Adam and Augustine. They knew what to
do and surmised that the King would want to hunt. Augustine
informed me that Burbage, their principal actor, wasn't yet with
them but that they had some of the King's Men who could sing

and dance. They couldn't at this stage mount a full play. But Robert Armin, a comic and singer, certainly could entertain the King. I realised that Armin was the diminutive man on the horse that I had seen arrive at Wilton.

"Any entertainment," I said, "Will have to do, if he wants it."

We had no indication of the time of the King's arrival but clearly, we needed to prepare the servants and the actors by telling them that visitors were expected. These visitors might want to hunt and certainly, they would want to eat, possibly staying for one night or more.

When Adam had gone, I said to Augustine,

"I wonder how many of them will come."

"No doubt we will be told at short notice." Augustine replied, adding "It will be interesting to see if H.W. comes."

"You mean W.H.?" I said.

"No," he replied. "H.W. Henry Wriothesley, the Earl of Southampton, whom I gather has been released from the Tower. The King seems to have forgiven him for his role with Essex in plotting a rebellion against the late Queen. He has now been welcomed back to court." I sat down, putting my head in my hands as I realised what was happening. I looked up,

"You mean that the two Earls, W.H. and H.W. will be here with Will at the same time?"

"Yes J.F.," he replied with a laugh, "It is as if they are mirrors of each other."

"So, when I look in a mirror my right side is my left and my left is my right?"

"That is correct," he laughed, "So W.H. and H.W. are like mirror images." With that he returned to the outhouses, still smiling at the idea.

As I later found out from Adam, the King was already thinking about moving from Theobalds, because of the plague. He and his courtiers were now looking at Winchester, and Wilton House in particular, for him to stay during the autumn and winter, rather than go back to Whitehall. The Scottish Gentlemen of the Bedchamber and other courtiers were to come to look at the estate for him and at the last minute, the King had decided to come with them since he needed to consider for himself whether it was a good enough Estate to go hunting. Also, Adam had told me that I would need to go to the cottage that day as the whole house could be taken over by the King's entourage at short notice.

I quite liked the idea of the isolation of the cottage on the grounds of the estate as it gave me my independence and Spikey the run of the fields. I got ready immediately and was taken by Adam to the place in question, some way out, at the edge of the forest. It couldn't even be seen from the house. Food and drink would be delivered to me daily and I had the opportunity to seek the company of the actors who had arrived from London and were now living in the outhouses. When we arrived at the cottage, Spikey and I thought that it was basic but habitable. I informed Amelia of my move and of my love. Spikey went in search of voles, mice and even rabbits.

CHAPTER 14

Before Jackie and Ever had left Oxford, Jennet Davenant had ensured that they both had clothes becoming to 'the times and the place'. Ever's own extravagant clothes needed to be destroyed, along with some of the garments and mock church vestments that Ever had been making. This was done through the judicial use of domestic fires when the tavern was empty.

Jackie and Ever used the new 'coach' service. As they approached the coach, two men who were getting off, saw their luggage and carried Ever's to the coach for her. They introduced themselves as Ben Jonson and Michael Drayton. "Not Jonson the dramatist?" said Ever.

"The same," Jonson replied. "I feel honoured that you know me." With that, the men left them to go on their way towards Stratford. Ever later told Jackie that she had never met Jonson at the Globe but had recognised him from the portrait back at home and the wart next to his nose!

They stopped, as arranged, at Shipston, where they had a warm welcome from Jennet's friend. That was Jackie's last day as a man and she felt a little sad, but a new life was beginning for the two women. Before leaving Shipston, Jackie left her masculine apparel in their room. The landlady would know what to do with it. The next morning, Ever and Jackie departed at dawn, as sisters-in-law. They boarded a horse and cart driven by another friend of Jennet's. For a cart, it was comfortable enough and fortunately, it was a bright sunny day.

They entered Stratford at Clopton Bridge and immediately saw Holy Trinity Parish Church in the distance on their left. Their instructions were to head for the Guild Chapel by the Guild Hall and the Grammar School, but when they reached Walkers Street there was a meat market still going on, with animals tethered up to the wall. They heard the cries of the animals waiting for death. The smell of it all was sickening to those not used to it. Still on the cart, they had to backtrack to Bridge Street and then turn left onto High Street and Chapel Street. Many people were out for market day so Jackie and Ever caused a bit of a stir. Ever played to the crowd, giving them a 'royal wave', whilst Jackie, somewhat embarrassed, kept telling her not to draw attention to themselves. Jackie, now being a woman of colour, preferred to keep a low profile. She knew there were always some in any community, who were prejudiced against 'aliens', ready to shout 'go back to where you've come from'.

Eventually, they reached the crossroad between Chapel Street and the other end of Walkers Street from where the smell of the animals being slaughtered and cut up as fresh meat was still appalling. It was on that corner, however, that the large house, New Place, was situated. They alighted and feeling somewhat sick rang a bell outside the main gate. The house didn't look in particularly good order. A maid answered. They told her that they had been sent by Jennet Davenant at the Salutation Tavern.

"Ah yes," said the servant, "Missus Shakespeare is expecting you." They later found out that Anne and Will had bought the house in quite a dilapidated state. What interested the Shakespeares was that it was not only a big house which could be made into a comfortable home fit for a gentleman and his wife, but that it had a garden for Mulberry trees, whose leaves were beloved by silkworms. The silk business, together with other cottage industries, were run by Mrs Shakespeare, although under Will's name. It brought in profits to the family, whilst her husband made an income, not only by working and acting in plays but through his investments. He also had stakes in The Globe and the indoor Blackfriars Theatre, so all his money could not go back to Stratford as he had loans to pay off.

Anne Shakespeare gave Jackie and Ever a warm welcome. She said that she'd heard about them from Jennet and that it had been her husband's idea to bring them up to Stratford, where they could work at New Place and be themselves, safe from more prying eyes. This perplexed Jackie and Ever. What did Mrs Shakespeare know? Anne said she wanted them to settle into the Stratford community as 'friends of Will from London.' She added that the plans had been worked out for some time.

"What do you mean?" Jackie protested.

"Don't be alarmed. William and Augustine put two and two together not long after your twin brother arrived in London. Will got him out into the countryside. We thought you were safe enough in Oxford but there are spies everywhere. They are searching for Catholic priests, who are dressed in many disguises. Indeed, you were almost compromised just before you left Oxford."

Ever responded, "Do you mean…?" but Anne interrupted her.

"No names please, but I gather it was a man sitting by the window."

CHAPTER 15

A t Wilton, I enjoyed the change brought about by the arrival of the actors. As I went to watch the rehearsals, I realised that there was also a corporate element to the writing, as not just one writer, but a number of writers would consider the text and then the actors would try things out, to see how they sounded and looked on stage. No one was frightened to change the script, although sometimes the writers would get upset if actors started to stray too far from what had been written for them. Nevertheless, the play was owned, as it were, by the company and by the actors working on it, not necessarily by the original writer. Shakespeare was nowhere to be seen at this point. He left the roles for the various actors in a new play, but they were still up for consideration during the rehearsals.

Spikey was more than happy with his life at Wilton. He and I were now close companions in a 'foreign land.' Some of the actors visited the cottage, with whom Spikey enjoyed playing and there was one in particular, Alfred, who was to play Isabella in *Measure for Measure*. This was one of the plays that they were starting to rehearse in the outhouses, in anticipation of a possible return to the Globe, once the plague was over.

Alfred's friendship with Spikey was something special to see. The two got on so well that they followed each other around. This also allowed me to get to know Alfred. As part of my quest, I needed to understand how the theatre worked and how it might change with the new Monarch. Where better to start than to talk to one of the boys about his experiences? For example, how did he come to work for the company?

Boys had to play the female parts because it was unlawful for men to dress as women, even on the stage and it was also illegal for women to appear on the public stage. This, of course, wasn't going to deter the King's wife, the Queen and her ladies, from appearing in elaborate masques at court or for rich ladies to do likewise in their wealthy homes, where they might even create their own plays for private performances. As in my own age, there was one rule for the rich and another for the poor.

But, how were young actors recruited? Alfred told me that some would be offloaded onto the company by grateful parents who were too poor to look after them. Others were pressed into acting or kidnapped by one or other of the theatre companies. They might even then be re-kidnapped by another company. But Alfred himself told me that Augustine had found him and his brother searching for food on the mud flats of the Thames in London. I was amazed and prompted the boy to give more details, asking about his parents and how he had ended up searching for food at the side of a filthy river.

I noticed that he was concentrating on something else, a plate of apples, which I had in the cottage. So, I asked him if he would like one. He nodded and took it, eating like someone who had known hunger. It disappeared in just a few seconds so I gave him another as he started his story.

His parents and sister had died of the plague and judging by his age I think he meant the one from 1593-5. Up until then, all had been well and they had been a happy family but sickness struck their home when he was about five years old. As soon as their parents and sister showed signs of having the illness, the three of them moved into one small room and blocked the door. The boys were told that they had to stay in the kitchen area so that those infected were isolated. The boys made food which they left outside their parents' door. Water with oats was all they could find. When neighbours suspected that plague was in the house, they boarded up the outside door and blocked all the openings, so that no one inside could escape. This meant that the boys had no access to wood to make a fire, though they did have tallow candles and a flint. There were a few slivers of light that came in through cracks in the walls, but not much. They called to their parents when food was ready and they'd put it outside their parent's room. Their parents would take the bowls and then return them empty. After a couple of days, they heard their parents crying, saying that their sister had died.

Soon after that, when they called out to their parents, there was no answer. No one came for the food. Alfred wanted to go into his parents' room but Nathan stopped him. They decided that they would have to leave the house in which they had been imprisoned. Nathan had suggested that perhaps they could set the house alight, using their flint, and then when people came to put the fire out, they could be rescued. But it was risky as maybe the neighbours would just leave the house to burn down. Alfred told his brother if rats and mice could get in and out, so could they. They felt all around the walls to see if there was a weakness. At the back, where the water was stored, it seemed that there was a softening in the wall. They started working on it with their bare hands and then they found an old blade and used that to open up a hole. Nathan gave up a couple of times, saying that they would never make a hole large enough to get through, but young Alfred insisted that they could get out. Eventually, they worked on the area and made a hole big enough to squeeze through. It was night and they took with them the flint, the blade and what was left of the oats. On leaving, they decided that they should burn the house down so that neighbours, thinking that they were all inside, would not realise that they had escaped. They put wood and dry leaves up against the wall of their house and used the flint to start a fire. As their home started to burn, they ran to hide among the trees and they watched as people gathered around in the dark and looked on, whilst the small building burned to the ground. No one tried to put the fire out, or even to check if anyone was alive inside.

The moon was shining as Nathan and Alfred made their way towards the river, which they followed towards London. There they scrounged and begged for food until Augustine found them and took them back to his home. He and his wife looked after them, as though they were their own.

It was an amazing story. I remembered Nathan from my previous visit to London and so I asked after him. I found out that he was touring with another section of the company led by Mr Burbage elsewhere in England. Alfred whispered,

"Nathan has a problem."

"What's that?" I asked.

"He's becoming a man," Alfred told me.

"Is he pleased about that?"

"I think so," Alfred said, "because then he'll be able to go with the girls like the other men do."

"Where do they go?"

"Mr Wilkins Tavern. They enjoy going there to see the women."

"How do you know?

"Oh, we've watched the women many times."

"How?"

Alfred looked at me with a grin and a wink and then he said wisely,

"If you know how to make a hole in the wall big enough to escape through, you can certainly make a small one to see through!" He laughed and took his leave. I went to get myself an apple but I noticed the dish was empty.

JOURNAL

I wondered whether the uncaring behaviour of the people in Alfred's village in times of crisis was typical. Not everyone behaves in an altruistic way but I can't help thinking that there would have been some of the villagers who would have wanted to help Alfred's family. The dominant wish, however, of the community did not allow them to follow their conscience. I recalled from my knowledge of history that around 1665/6 there was a village called Eyam in Derbyshire which was visited by the plague. It may have come into the village via a package, which was delivered to the local tailor. As people began to die, the minister at the local church brought the community together and they imposed a virtual lockdown within the village. The dead were buried immediately by their families. There were to be no group meetings, not even in the church. The inhabitants agreed not to leave their village. Food was brought from other villages and left outside Eyam's boundaries. The inhabitants effectively isolated their village until the plague receded. Many in the community died, but their actions helped to limit the spread of the plague. It was a community endeavour, which showed that they cared about their fellow human beings.

When in my own time COVID struck the U.K. there were workers in care homes, where COVID was rife, who remained in their places of work for several weeks, rather than going back and forth to their own homes and running the risk of spreading the disease. This was in contrast to some others who saw this new plague as a means of making vast sums of money, for example by selling worthless so-called personal protective equipment which proved to be unusable. There were many rumours of corruption and I have no reason to contradict these. Evidence was given to a later public inquiry that the Prime Minister and some of his cabinet would have been content to let the old people to die to protect the economy, exposing their mantra of money first, and people second.

CHAPTER 16

W hen Perry turned up for his next appointment, a new Prime Minister, Charles Pritchard had been elected. Most of the press seemed to have lost interest in pursuing Perry on a range of issues, at least for the time being, owing to their focus on that election. But one female TV journalist, Helena Rousseau, kept asking questions about Perry's finances within a larger discussion about corruption within his Party. Perry thought that maybe she was going after him because following the early death of her lover, the former Prime Minister, she too, was frustrated at not getting a peerage. He believed that she had a grudge against the Party and was setting out to embarrass them.

On his arrival, Amelia immediately noticed that Peregrine was immaculately dressed, indeed meticulously so, with a shiny black suit, white shirt, political party tie, and patent leather shoes. His hair was smartly combed flat, his face newly shaven and by the pungent smell in the room, clearly finished off with an expensive aftershave. He seemed to need, in his appearance, a recognition of his importance. But for all the care he had taken, his clothes still didn't quite fit.

"Do you wish me to start?" asked Perry pompously. This made Amelia smile to herself. But she said,

"Please do."

"I have been considering my former testimony to you and I have decided that I am in the right. I have not been cursed by the outpouring and threats of a demented female. I merely suffered a series of unfortunate coincidences. I am now held in high regard by the new Prime Minister. Indeed, I loaned him £80,000 to help him to realise his position of becoming the new P.M. I am not, however, in his Cabinet at the moment. The new P.M. assured me that at the first opportunity, I would be elevated to the House of Lords. That is why the witch's curse no longer affects me. I think the curse was all in the widow's mind, not mine. She was just trying to scare me. She has now disappeared from my life and indeed from public view."

He paused to check that Amelia was listening. "I am attending the House of Commons regularly. Indeed, only yesterday I tabled a question to the Prime Minister, which would have been taken, the Speaker informed me, if time had permitted."

He adjusted the knot in his tie before adding, "As you may be aware, I have just had a significant birthday, on which I was woken by a Salvation Army band, in full uniform, playing *Happy Birthday* outside my house. This was followed by *Land of Hope and Glory*. The neighbours in Palm Avenue all thought it was wonderful, except the man at number 79, who complained vociferously that he worked nights and had been trying to get to sleep. Mind you, my wife Camilla, tells me that his wife Tracy puts out their washing on the line and leaves the pegs on it all the time, even after their underwear has been removed! Underwear on the line, I ask you! So common. They are completely the wrong sort for our Avenue, but there are some things we have to endure.

I am now in a good place. As I mentioned, I do not believe I was cursed. I think it was just the anger of a misguided, grieving widow, who had discovered the truth about her late husband. I therefore wish to inform you that I no longer need your services."

Amelia replied that she was pleased that Sir Peregrine was in a good place but to let her know if he needed to see her in future. With that, she showed him out of the consulting room. As Peregrine left, he stumbled and in righting himself, he put his hands to his head to ensure that his hair was still in place. Amelia thought that maybe his façade was cracking slightly. As she went back to her room, she said to Dafydd,

"He'll be back before long. By the way, is his wife really called Camilla?"

"I don't think so," he replied, "It was Gladys when they got married. But, of course, we do have a new King!"

CHAPTER 17

O ne rather bright day, when I was back at my cottage, Alfred came in and started our conversation with, "Were you ever an actor?"

"I like theatre," I replied, "But as for acting I was not born for that profession." Alfred laughed as Spikey jumped up onto his lap.

"Do you think that I was?" he asked, whilst stroking the cat.

"You perform as if you were," I replied, "But your history has helped your imagination and that has honed your skills." He considered that I was probably right. The way in which his mother, father and sister had died had haunted him throughout his young life, but he acknowledged the kindness of Augustine who had rescued him and Nathan. Alfred asked quietly,

"How could people be so cruel and so frightened of us, that they might have set fire to a house in which people were alive and then do nothing to try to save them?"

"I can't answer that question except by saying that people can be desperately cruel to one another, to the point of killing each other or watching others die for their own amusement." Alfred was munching on some nuts listening intently to me. I added, "Previous rights and wrongs held in your memory can be used in the roles that you might portray on stage,"

He said he thought he understood what I was saying. Recently he has been playing the role of Viola in *Twelfth Night*. It was rumoured that the King might wish to see it, here in Wilton, but no one was sure where he might be at any time. Taking more nuts from the dish Alfred commented that it wasn't easy playing a girl, who had to dress up as a boy, just to survive in life.

He said, "I mean, what if you were a girl and were having to play a boy, wouldn't you find that odd? You'd be mixing up boys and girls in your head. Girls don't always act like boys and vice versa. I have to think, when playing Viola as being a girl and her dressing as a boy, like me, but still being enough of a girl to entice the Duke to fall in love with me. He should not do so, as he is a man and he should love a woman, not another man or boy. Does that make sense?" I said that it did but that for many people it's only a comedy to amuse them.

"But that's the point," he said. "Since as a boy, after having been a girl, I might love the Duke as a boy." He looked at me with a worried expression on his face.

"Are you asking me, Alfred, why a man can't love a man?" He remained silent for a while before saying,

"Yes."

"And are you asking because you feel love for a man or another boy, not only in the play but perhaps outside it in real life?" He remained silent but I noticed he was no longer eating. He just sat there looking out the window, with Spikey in his arms. There was something on his mind.

"Has anyone tried to seduce you?" I asked.

He looked up at me in horror. "No, no." He said, putting the cat down. "That hasn't happened. Of course, there are men, who when the play is over, try to fondle you, but we get away from them." He looked away from the window and back to me.

"I think I'm attracted to someone," he said slowly.

"And is he attracted to you?"

"Maybe," the boy replied.

"And is that what you use to draw on in your performance when Cesario is with Orsino?"

"Perhaps it's that which had made me think about it."

"Let me tell you", I said. "In the place and time I come from, some men love men and some men love women. Likewise, some women love women and some women love men. Some people feel that although they might have been born physically female, they feel they are male and vice versa. We understand that it has to do with the complexity of each individual's makeup both physically and mentally. Therefore, I am used to knowing men who are in love with other men, women with other women and indeed people wishing to change sex. We have medical ways which may allow this to happen. But in the time in which you are living, there is prejudice and misunderstanding of the nature of love, as it varies from one individual to another. The Church condemns it, as does the country. So, you need to take care of what you say and how you act. It is dangerous, Alfred, but your feelings are your own and you should not allow others to tell you how to feel. What you should worry about is the condemnation by others and in that, I can give you no help except to say people can be vicious."

Alfred said he wished he had lived in my age and then he said quietly that maybe he shouldn't have told me. I replied that what was said between me and a client didn't go any further for either of us. He smiled but then asked me whether I knew that the new King, so people say, sleeps with men. I replied that I had heard the rumours, but maybe it was tittle-tattle that could get people into trouble and we shouldn't be talking about it.

"But isn't that wrong?" he said. "If he sleeps with men, how can he execute men for sleeping with each other? That is horrible!"

"That Alfred is power. One rule for the people but another

for the rulers. That is one thing that is wrong in many societies".

He nodded saying, "I like talking to you – but I don't love you," he added with a laugh. He took some more nuts and said he would see me again sometime for another chat. Then he went running back to the outhouses and the other actors.

JOURNAL

Why do individuals search for power? Is it in their genetic makeup? Some get pleasure and sexual satisfaction when they exercise power, enjoying the feeling of superiority and developing a need for more.

How do people feel when they have power? A tyrant over the people? The King over the kingdom? The Pope over the church? The priest over the congregation? A teacher over the pupils? An employer over the employees? A man over a woman or a woman over a man?

I once met a man, who had been wounded in the war. He had been offered a promotion at work, which would mean more money and greater perks, but he turned it down because of the old saying that 'power tends to corrupt and absolute power corrupts absolutely.' He said that he wanted to be as he was and had no ambition to be 'in charge' of anyone. This man had seen how those in power used it for their own benefit and aggrandisement, whilst others died in the trenches.

But if no one is in charge, how can we, as a society, organise ourselves? We need our hierarchies but the trick is how to ensure that those at the bottom have an equal value to those at the top. If I could solve that problem, maybe I could be the next great political leader! But then would power insidiously corrupt me too?

CHAPTER 18

In early autumn 1604, within my cottage on the Wilton estate, I noticed that the standard of food had gone up to another level. I suspected that the King may have arrived, or was about to do so. I was getting the leftovers, of course, but certainly, there was a difference. On a number of days, I could hear the hunt in the distance. On one rather cold day in particular, it happened to come close to my cottage and the King, in his enthusiasm, rode his horse past an overhanging branch, which clipped him. He fell and the horse galloped on. His closest riding companion helped him up and seeing my cottage brought him here to shelter. The King was protesting that he wasn't hurt but there was a gash on his forehead. His young companion ordered me out of the cottage but the King saw me and said,

"No, leave the peasant alone. He may stay." His companion patched him up but the King kept looking at me and signalled that I should come closer to him. He was now sitting near to the fire. It was then that my adventure changed. He looked me up and down and asked if I were the black man working in the theatre. I answered respectfully that I was working with what I understood to be the King's Men.

"So, you are the 'mind doctor' about whom I've heard some stories?" he inquired.

"Well, I call myself a psychotherapist which is someone helping the mind".

"And where do you come from?" he asked. But before I could answer he said.

"Tell me no lies since I've been talking with Pembroke about you. You are particularly handsome." I hesitated, deciding to ignore this last remark and I told him that I came from the future.

Having possibly misunderstood me, he replied, "I don't need the name of your house, but rather I want to know more about you."

"There is not much to tell," I said. "My name is Dr Jacob Fortune. I'm a psychotherapist or 'mind doctor' and I'm a partner in a company called *4 Psychotherapists 4 U*. My premises are a long way from here."

"Are you a madman?" he asked.

"No," I answered. "I try to help people not to go mad."

"Pembroke and that dramatist fellow speak highly of you. I'm glad I've met you." He held out his hand with the coronation ring upon it. I knelt and kissed it as was expected. "You may take your leave," he said. I thought that this meant that I was to go outside and so I went to the door. He laughed and said, "No, I will go and you stay here in your cottage." He continued to laugh to himself as he and his companion went to leave the room. He then suddenly turned and asked,

"Jacob, who is the Monarch in your country?"

"It was Her Majesty Queen Elizabeth ll, who was greatly loved but sadly she has died whilst I have been out here. She has been succeeded by her eldest son, now King Charles III."

"Charles III," he replied thoughtfully. "And is he loved?"

"I think so, Sir, almost as much as you are," he smiled.

"Thank you," he said." You are very polite for a black man."

He mounted his horse, which had been brought to him and then turned in his saddle and said to me "Pembroke was correct, you are handsome." With that, he and his companion were gone.

"Did that really happen?" I asked Spikey, as he came in from outside with a vole in his mouth, which he deposited at my feet. "I take that to be a 'yes'." Spikey just purred.

JOURNAL

Later it turned out that the Scottish King was particularly suspicious of those who professed a knowledge of the future. In his mind, they were linked to witches, magic and black people and needed to be dealt with appropriately. Fortunately, he thought I'd given him the name of my house or he had misheard me. I needed to be more careful in what I said or I would find myself in trouble. But his appearance at my cottage had taken me off guard.

CHAPTER 19

Two days after the King had been to my cottage, I woke up with a start. It had been a cold moonlit night and I had lost my cover so I was lying naked on my mattress. I turned to the window and saw someone looking at me. I'd never thought of the lack of privacy in my bedroom before, because no one ever came round here. The person did not try to hide but rather stood back from the window. There was no doubt, it was the King.

I got up from my bed. "My Lord," I said.

"Your Majesty," he corrected me but then said that he would come in. I was naked in his full view, of course. I reached for a garment to put on before I went to the front door.

"I'm aware it is early," the King said. "But I wanted to meet you without too many people around. I have my guards, of course, within easy distance, to help me should I need protection."

"Protection from whom Your Majesty?" I asked.

"Why, you, of course. I have no real knowledge about who you are or what you are, except…." and he laughed, "that you are certainly a man!" So, the voyeur had come to the peasant, I thought.

I knew exactly what he was wanting but I decided to distract him and said, "Would you like to sit down, Your Majesty?" He did so. "I wondered whether you would like to talk about yourself." (I knew this was his favourite subject.)

"You mean, try your psycho something or other? Your mind-talk?"

I immediately corrected him by saying, "They are not *my* mind talks, Your Majesty. I listen, whilst my client talks in order to relieve the pressures of the mind."

"But is what is said in confidence?" he asked.

"Your majesty, I have to make notes, of course, which are locked away, but all is confidential within this room." He thought for a while and then he said that I was particular with my words. He realised that Pembroke had said that I was from a distant place. He continued,

"Before you live, you have no life and after you live, your life is with God."

I responded that such was the belief of Christians. I didn't wish to get into a conversation about religion, but rather I wanted him to talk about himself.

"So, Your Majesty," I asked him. "Are you interested in mind talk?"

"Why do you think I am here?"

"It's not my job to speculate. I listen, Your Majesty. Through listening I help." I then remained silent.

"Are you not going to ask a question?" He asked, but I kept quiet. He didn't speak for some time but rather he just looked round the room. He then stood up and walked to the bedroom, opened the door and looked in. I remained seated although, in royal etiquette, that would not have been permitted. If the King stood, you stood – but I didn't. He was my client, whether a King, a Pope, or an actor, all would receive the same professional attention. But let's be frank, to have stood as he went to the bedroom could have proved more dangerous for me. He returned and sat down. Then he began,

"I've seen people of your colour before – even darker and blacker than you. It is the devil's colour you know." I remained silent, knowing that he was challenging me.

"You are all of one colour from head to foot. I saw you this morning." He paused. "I once had four of your kind dancing in the snow, wearing no clothes. My wife and I watched them from our carriage in Copenhagen. They danced and danced alongside us. We laughed to see them in their nakedness. As they became more and more tired, their dances slowed. The slave master then whipped them until they found new energy to dance as the snow was falling. We became bored with them, watching their nakedness swinging with their dance. But still they danced and when we reached the palace, they died. They fell into the snow, with no one of their kind to pick them up. After we had gone indoors, their carcasses were removed. You reminded me of them this morning when I saw you in your nakedness." He hesitated. "You interest me. Do you think that is sinful?"

I needed to maintain a distance, so I said quietly,

"I am not a priest, Your Majesty, so I do not regard my clients as a priest would his parishioners. I listen but what is important is that you can say whatever is on your mind. You have done that. It is not for me to have views about what you say. If you wish to talk about it, that is your prerogative. That is what helps the mind."

"People don't usually talk to me in that way," he said. "Are you not concerned that I can just call out and guards will come in here to silence you forever? I don't understand what you do but I'll think about what you have said. I am a powerful man and I can use people as I want. It is my gift from God himself. Authority, power, deciding what is right and what is wrong. That is all in my hands, not yours. What else do you know about me?"

"You Majesty, that is not for me to say, but you are my King." I answered.

He repeated, "I could have you silenced in an instant. Do you understand?" He paused before saying, "But what good would that do?" He looked at me and smiled. "I may come again," he said and with that, he left my cottage. I gave a sigh of relief. I was intrigued by the man, but at the same time, I was frightened by his power and by the way he looked at me.

I sought out Augustine and told him about the visit. He advised that I should keep to the cottage and say nothing. The King would be returning to London soon. He realised that I was frightened by the visit.

Some days later, I heard that the King had left Wilton and so I went for a long walk through the woods. I found the carcass of a small fawn that had been hunted down and left by the huntsmen. It must have been too small for a feast. I sat by it, with the rain seeping through the trees and onto my head and clothes. I felt like the fawn, but although threatened, at least I had survived. I was better off than this little carcass.

When I returned to my cottage, I found that glass had been fitted into my little window in the bedroom and also into the window in the main room. Furthermore, drapes had been hung around my bed. I asked the servant Adam, who had brought my afternoon meal, where these alterations had come from. He said that the Earl, who had left with the King, had ordered this to be done. I realised that I was to stay in my cottage for the winter months.

Did the King come to my cottage again? Was he still intrigued by me and by my colour? Had I become a source of his imagination and of his desire? Did he contemplate being with me, relieving his troubled mind and fantasy? I cannot answer. It would be dangerous to narrate. If I were a victim and caused trouble, I wouldn't be the only one to suffer. It would rebound on others, such as Shakespeare and the Earl of Pembroke. I said and wrote nothing. Maybe he didn't come to the cottage again.

Earlier in the year, two Catholic priests had attempted to

assassinate the King in a rather botched job known as the Bye plot. This trial led to the discovery of another plot, the Main plot, in which Lord Cobham and Sir Walter Raleigh with others appeared to have been involved. It was treachery and Cobham, to save his neck, accused Raleigh. Yet no sooner had he done so than he recanted. It was too late. Raleigh was to be tried and with London still in the midst of the plague, the trial took place in Winchester.

The people had been stirred up against Raleigh, just as in my own times when someone of great regard falls from power, they get ridiculed in the media. When Raleigh went to his trial in 1603, people lined the streets, shouting abuse at him and pelting him with mud and muck. Yet only months before he had led the procession of the soldiers at the Queen's funeral. The populace can be persuaded by propaganda to turn against men of power and influence and often don't realise that behind closed doors envy reigns and plots are hatched for revenge to be taken. In this case, persons of influence were listening and manoeuvring in secret, because a popular Raleigh could have been a danger. A dead one would be history.

That November, Cobham and Raleigh were to be tried in Winchester. The King and his court came back to stay at Wilton House. I later discovered that the Scottish King was looking forward to another voyeuristic adventure, this time in the courtroom

I understood from the gossip that the King was travelling daily from Wilton, to attend the trial, in secret. He listened to the proceedings from behind a wooden partition. What he must have heard was an aggressive Sir Edward Coke, the Attorney General, insisting on Raleigh's involvement in the Main Plot, as evidenced by Lord Cobham's allegations. He would have heard Raleigh's statement that Cobham had rescinded his allegations and should be brought to court, to confirm that renunciation. Coke did not allow this to happen. Raleigh spoke eloquently in his own defence. Coke made the accusations but was no orator.

However, he was determined that Raleigh should be convicted. Coke was basically a bully, who in other circumstances would have had no qualms about using torture to get a confession. He couldn't do that in court, so he bullied Raleigh with words. The King heard it all. The jury was asked to make a decision and with little deliberation, they found Raleigh guilty. He was condemned to death and the date of December 11th was set for his execution. The King secretly wrote a reprieve, which he cruelly ordered to be delivered the day before the execution. Thereby Raleigh was spared at the last minute but subsequently had to languish in the Tower of London for nigh on 14 years. In 1616 he was released to go on a voyage to the newly discovered lands, to find gold for the realm. It was an El Dorado Expedition that went badly, resulting in him attacking the Spanish in violation of a peace treaty signed by the Scottish King. On his return, the sentence of the 1603 trial was reinstated and Coke at last saw the Great Nobleman executed in 1618. Raleigh was embalmed and his head was kept in a red leather bag by his widow until she died nearly 30 years later in 1647.

What did the Scottish King think while indulging in his voyeuristic pleasure behind the panels of the courtroom? Did he enjoy hearing the eloquent denial and the unjust verdict given? Did he realise that Coke was lacking evidence, deliberately keeping Cobham away from the trial? Did the King wallow in the knowledge that Raleigh did not know until the last minute that he had been reprieved?

I wondered about the King and his voyeurism. He could have changed the verdict and insisted that the charge was trumped up. He could have spared Raleigh then and there but he did neither. He just allowed him to remain in captivity. With voyeurism, there is often sadism.

The King had spoken to Pembroke about my bedroom and the need for glass and drapes. Why was that I wondered? Perhaps he was, as people reported, just a feather in the wind, unsettled and drifting from one situation to another, selfishly, privately, enjoying his exercise of power, or perhaps he just didn't like the cold!

JOURNAL

Psychotherapy does not in itself protect you from your clients. They can become attracted to you but just as easily they can be envious and aggressive because you have seen them at their weakest point. There are still things that occur, some conversations that happen, words that are uttered which are of such privacy, that they cannot be recorded. This is why it is important for psychotherapists to have regular sessions with their supervisors.

On a happier note, I had a message from Amelia. In late October Dafydd had booked a holiday, in expectation of the birth of the new baby. He and Maddie had moved into a larger apartment, not far from the Practice, where they had an ideal room for a nursery. Dafydd decorated the whole flat, including the nursery ready for the arrival of the girl or boy – they decided they didn't want to know which. There was teddy bear wallpaper and spacecraft craft balloons, plus a quote from Mr Shakespeare,

'Tis a lucky day… and we'll do good deeds on't.

It would indeed be a lucky day for them. Dafydd was up a step ladder, finishing work on the bathroom ceiling, when Maddie burst in and said that she thought the baby was on its way. He came down the ladder as fast as he could, putting his foot into the bucket of paint that he had left at the bottom!

"That's good luck," he said, whipping off his sock and grabbing another before getting Maddie to the hospital. She was in labour for some time, but all was well and in the early hours of the morning she gave birth to a little girl, whom they called Angela, after my wife Dr. Amelia Angel.

Messages were sent to me at Wilton House and to Jackie and

Ever in Stratford. Although we were all separated from one another, we celebrated this lovely day, which of course we still commemorate every year. Indeed, on Angela's birthday each year, the story of the painted sock is told. Dafydd framed the sock and hung it on the bathroom wall that he had been decorating. It was a good sock, a perfect sock but not as perfect as little Angela.

CHAPTER 20

I heard from Pembroke, that the King had been very taken with me during his time at Wilton House. I was still in the cottage as I had been throughout the summer, with the actors staying in the outhouses. They had given a performance in September of *As You Like It* in the gardens of the Estate with young Alfred taking the role of Rosalind and a boy named Nicholas taking the role of Celia. They were both excellent. The Earl had opened the grounds for the public and there was a good crowd to watch. A few of the actors then left to tour elsewhere.

Without telling me what he was up to, Augustine called a meeting with the company in one of the barns used for rehearsals at Wilton House and he invited me to attend. The actors had decided that they wanted to work on a new play that would be staged the following year. At the end of the current year, they were going to conclude their time at Wilton House with a performance of *Twelfth Night*. If possible, this would take place on Christmas Day. But word came from Pembroke that he was required by the King and would now be at Court. The King had gone back to London as the plague had subsided. The actors were told that they would have to stay until January 1604. Pembroke suggested that *Twelfth Night* should be performed on the twelfth night of Christmas in the Great Hall when he could attend with his guests. Everyone was pleased about this. There wasn't much need for a detailed rehearsal of this play as the actors had been performing it since before the death of Queen Elizabeth.

They needed a new play to perform once the new season started in the following spring. Will had drafted much of a new one about a black General, Othello, who falls in love with Desdemona, the white daughter of Brabantio, a Venetian Senator.

Augustine explained the plot to us all saying,

"Brabantio objects strongly to the relationship between Othello and Desdemona, which had been revealed to him by a frustrated and evil soldier called Iago. Othello trusts Iago but Iago is jealous of him. The Senate, however, is preoccupied with a Turkish attack on their colony of Cyprus. Othello, as their General, needs to be sent to defeat the Turks. It is revealed that Othello and Desdemona are already married. The Senators, therefore, turn down Brabantio's objections and Othello is commissioned to sail for Cyprus. Desdemona pleads to go with him and permission is given but she has to sail on a different boat. Iago, frustrated in his first attempt to deceive Othello, sees an opportunity in Cyprus to try again. He sows the seed in Othello's mind, that Desdemona is having an affair with another officer named Cassio. In a mad fit of jealousy, Othello murders Desdemona and when Iago's evil is revealed, the black General kills himself."

The actors agreed that it was a very different play from *Twelfth Night*! They were happy to go back to a tragedy for the new season. How better than to start rehearsals at Wilton?

Augustine gave out some of the key roles to the company. Alfred, who had been given the part of Desdemona, called out, "Mr Burbage isn't here so who will take Othello's role?"

"Yes, who is taking the part of Othello? You didn't give his role out." I asked.

"Didn't I?" Augustine said with false sincerity. "In that case, it has to be you, Jacob, doesn't it, since you are the only black man here." Everyone laughed, except me, as he gave me the roll of paper with a wink, saying quietly, "Now it's your turn to play with The King's Men." What could I do? It was an honour that my friend Augustine had given me. I looked over a speech that came towards the end of the play. It was one I had read so many times that it was already imprinted on my mind.

"This looks like a good speech," I said, "It comes before he kills his wife." I began,

It is the cause, it is the cause, my soul:
Let me not name it to you, you chaste stars:
It is the cause. Yet I'll not shed her blood,
Nor scar that whiter skin of hers than snow,
And smooth as monumental alabaster:
Yet she must die, else she'll betray more men.
Put out the light, and then put out the light.

You could hear a pin drop in the barn where we were rehearsing as I went through the speech and together, Alfred and I continued to act out the story of Desdemona's death.

"You're some actor, Jacob," Alfred said to me as we were applauded.

"You certainly are." Augustine laughed. "You'd better not let Burbage know when he returns. It's his role." Of course, it was and, of course, I knew they were being generous, but I felt elated, not only by my performance, but by the warmth and kindness of this theatrical company, known as The King's Men.

CHAPTER 21

The 'Christmas' performance of *Twelfth Night* at Wilton House as planned, took place on twelfth night itself. W.H. had granted permission that as part of the fun, the servants in the house could, if they wished, follow the tradition of the 'feast of fools,' by cross-dressing: the men dressing as women, the women as men. It would all add to the festivity. The King, who had held court at Wilton through November, had long since returned to London. So, Wilton House was able to relax and be itself again. Before the performance, there was a banquet. I was honoured to be on the guest list, even though I was still living at the cottage. I was excited to go as a guest. It meant, however, that I didn't need to attend in women's clothes. A cross-dressing man of colour might have been just a little too much even for their twelfth night. More importantly, it would have drawn too much attention to me.

What I found was that I was joining a literary circle. This included W.H.'s mother, Mary Sidney as was, until she married the second Earl of Pembroke. She was intellectually an independent woman, the sister of the poet Philip Sidney, and a great patron of the arts. I was presented to her almost as if she were the Queen herself, with whom, I later discovered, she was friends. I looked around the room at the gathering, which included poets, entrepreneurs, dramatists, and actors. It was an array of talent but to my excitement, there was also, at last, the Earl of Southampton, Henry Wriothesley, in attendance. Was that political? Of course, it was. Everything with these aristocrats was political and there was even a competitiveness about their interest in the arts. W.H. had failed to get the King to return to Wilton House, so soon after Raleigh's trial. Similarly, the Queen, who was a patron of the arts, was also absent. W.H., nevertheless, would have been very much aware that the Queen had been to a performance of *Love's Labour's Lost* at Southampton's house but had had to decline the invitation to Wilton House. No doubt Southampton had noticed this. The Queen had promised to come at a later date. Despite there being a competition for royal favour, today Southampton was the honoured guest and I could see the two of them, W.H. and H.W., in earnest conversation with no other than Will Shakespeare. But which of the two, was the Mr W.H. of the sonnets?

I knew most of the people only from history and I recognised an Italian, John Florio, who had translated Montaigne, who was talking to the red-headed 'young Turk' John Marston. Marston was being teased over an argument he'd had with Ben Jonson, which had led to a challenge from Jonson. Marston denied that Jonson had been the victor.

"Not so, not so," the young Marston laughed. Looking around the room he said satirically,

"Where is Jonson? I see no Jonson. I hear no Jonson. I spy no Jonson. But shush, maybe he is in Rome." There was laughter all around because Jonson's allegiance to the Church of Rome was well known.

"It will backfire on him eventually." Southampton laughed.

"No!" retorted Marston. "Jonson will turn to the King's

Church, mark my words, once he sees the way the world is going under His Majesty's firm hand. Then he quoted from one of his own plays, saying,

"What religion are you?" with the answer,

"Why of the King's religion, when I know which it is!"

Will interjected. "Be careful, Marston. Walls have ears. But how about a song from tonight's play?"

With that, they called for Robert Armin to sing:

Come away, come away, death,
And in sad cypress let me be laid.
Fly away, fly away, breath,
I am slain by a fair cruel maid.
My shroud of white, stuck all with yew,
O, prepare it!
My part of death, no one so true
Did share it.

W.H. led the applause, laughing that you could always rely on Armin to sing a 'jolly song'! Then he said, "I gather we will hear it again in the play which I understand is to commence at the far end of the Hall."

At last, I was able to see the King's Men in *Twelfth Night*. Alfred's performance as Viola was extremely good, especially in his scenes with Orsino, in which his love for the Duke was summed up in his story of a sister, who never told of her love,

"But let concealment, like a worm in the bud feed on her damask cheek... "

"But," Orsino asked, "died thy sister of her love, my boy?" To which Alfred replied,

"I am all the daughters of my father's house and all the brothers too and yet I know not."

I noticed that Pembroke's mother, Mary Sydney, listening intently, smiled sadly and I surmised that maybe she was thinking of her lost brother.

After the performance, I met Marston, who said, "I wish I could write as well as Will Shakespeare." I was surprised at his modesty.

"You don't do too badly," I replied.

"That's because Will tutored me and I don't mind anyone knowing that to be true." I thought I'd try my luck and probed, asking him which of the Earls, W.H. or H.W. did Shakespeare most favour.

"Oh," he said tapping his nose "the one he loves the best." He laughed and went off to talk with some others but as we mingled a man came up to me and asked if he could have a word. He introduced himself as Michael Drayton. I shook his hand. I'd wondered whether it might be the poet. As it happened, I had a quote ready from one of his poems,

'Since there's no help, come let us kiss and part / Nay, I have done, you get no more of me. '

He was delighted.

"How do you know that poem of mine?"

"Because I've read it," I replied. He laughed and thanked me but taking me aside, said that he had been in Oxford with Ben Jonson a few months ago, where he had seen me and my wife, Ever.

"You should have introduced yourself." I retorted.

He looked at me quizzically.

"Well, you may remember Jonson did say something, but we had just arrived. The odd thing is Jacob, that looking at you, I can't help noticing that you are not quite the same here as you were there."

"Well, I can assure you," I said, "That I am me wherever I am." I laughed.

Drayton then went on to say, "It is good to meet you. But there is no appetite for Violas and Cesarios or women dressed as men under the law. It would be unwise for you to draw too much attention to yourself. You must work out who and where you are!" I thanked him for his advice.

Later I asked Will about him. He said that he was a good friend and a respected poet but was known to be a Roman Catholic. It was then that he also told me that I needed to pack my possessions and prepare Spikey for a journey as we were all returning to London in a few days.

CHAPTER 22

As Amelia had predicted, an agitated Perry rang Dafydd for an appointment. He said that he had an ailment that he needed to discuss with Amelia.

He arrived in the consulting room wearing gloves and was shaking as he sat down.

"I was wrong," he said. "I am still cursed. I have blisters all over my hands. I have been to the doctor several times, but nothing he has given me has helped. My physician concluded it was psychosomatic and that my physical symptoms were caused by my mind and emotions. He advised me to see a psychotherapist."

"So, you wish to have another session with me?" She asked. This prompted the rude response,

"I have no confidence in you, but I am doing as my physician has suggested. Apparently, you are well known in professional circles, but I don't know why."

Amelia sat silently, waiting.

After some time, he began, "I had better tell you. I have some dreadful news, but this is in confidence. You will recall that I loaned £80,000 to the Prime Minister, Charles Pritchard. How could I have known that it was a personal loan? I thought

I was loaning it at the time, to help him get elected to be our next Prime Minister. How could I have known that he was a gambling addict? How could I have known that he would gamble it all away in a poker game with some Sheik from the Middle East at which a member of the Royal Family was also present? It is a disaster. The new P.M. is about to be outed and sacked and both the Party Chairman and my wife are furious with me for lending him the money. It actually belonged to my wife and had come from her shares in the tropical fish business."

Amelia was puzzled and interrupted him saying,

"Could you repeat that please?"

"Certainly. The money wasn't mine. It came from my wife's interest in the fish company."

Amelia smiled to herself, thinking that the tables had started to turn on this pompous little man and the political party to which he belonged. But of course, she said nothing.

Perry continued,

"How can I now make it to the House of Lords? I'm sure this P.M. will not be allowed an honours list. Pritchard may even go to prison. Did you know that the awful woman from the television, Helena Rousseau, is investigating the whole affair and for some reason has been asking questions about my brother-in-law's shares in the tropical fish company and other offshore investments? How should I know what shares he has? After all, he is the Chairman of the Party. What should I know about his dealings with the Russians? I never went to Russia even though I'd been invited. How did I know that their President was interested in fish – dead or alive?"

Ignoring the tirade, Amelia said quietly, "But I thought it was the late Prime Minister's wife who had shares in the tropical fish business."

To which he replied with exasperation, "Everyone in the government seems to have had shares in it. It was a worldwide cover. They were playing the markets everywhere with everyone. That is why I went to so many countries, doing their dirty business in a huge scam. It wasn't just the P.M.'s wife, but a whole group of them. I was on the outside, making various contacts in this country, all because they were avoiding leaving records on phones or the Internet. Then after I'd said what I'd been told to say by my colleagues, I came home with the results from the investigation about tropical fish. I was a fool, but I'd been promised a place in the House of Lords. I didn't find out what I'd actually been doing until after the late P.M. had his heart attack. I had tried to persuade him with the letter about his private life, but I was sitting on a much bigger issue – and it would be me at whom they would point the finger. I was completely duped by my own corrupt political friends. Some friends! In the past, I've always known what to do. Maybe I need to remove myself from the public arena for a time to 'spend time with my family'. I've been advised by the mandarins of my party that that will be the best way." He paused and then went on, "Or rather the usual way. It is a good idea. I know several Members of Parliament in my party who do not attend the House of Commons nor do they hold their constituency surgeries and yet they still get paid."

He thought about it again for a while before exclaiming, "No, damn it. I am not corrupt. I am going to fight. I'll do what ministers do regularly and deny everything. But I'll be revenged on the whole pack of them unless I am made a Lord."

With that, he abruptly got up and left without even saying goodbye to Amelia.

When Dafydd saw Peregrine striding out of the Practice, he came into Amelia's room and asked,

"Do you think that is the last we will see of him?"

"I hope so. He is up to date with his payments, isn't he?"

"Of course, Amelia," replied Dafydd smiling.

CHAPTER 23

Some days after twelfth night, Spikey and I returned to London with the players. When we arrived, I resumed my lease at The Elephant and checked that all was well in the consulting room. Everything was as it should be. I was concerned about Michael Drayton's warning to me about Jackie and Ever, but I knew from Amelia, that they were still in lodgings at New Place in Stratford with Anne Shakespeare. More importantly, they were now both in female dress, as sisters-in-law, Jackie and Ever Fortune.

I thought back to the Wilton House party and performance. I'd watched both Earls closely. It seemed to me that they were not mirror images. W.H. was a more politically astute character than Southampton but did that make him a greater candidate than the other to be Mr W.H.? Both of them had supported Shakespeare in his work.

Alfred came round to see me but in talking of men dressing as women and vice versa, he let slip that there had been a rumour that I was a woman.

"When was that?" I laughed.

"It started just before Ever left," he replied. "I miss Ever."

"But who was talking about me being a woman?"

"Oh, it was just a silly rumour that went around, but Augustine put a stop to it."

"How did he do that?"

Alfred laughed and said, "Augustine told us that you and he had had a pee together one day and it was clear that you were not female." I thought back to the time when I had been on a walk with Augustine and we had looked on some bushes, so to speak. The rumour however may have got out of hand, if Augustine had not intervened.

I wrote to Amelia.

Dearest Amelia,

It is a quiet time after the Christmas festivities. I am concerned, that although Jackie and Ever are now in Stratford, some rumours went about at Wilton House which may still cause some difficulty. I wonder if they should return home.

Love Jacob

The response came,

My dearest Jacob,

As far as your worry is concerned Ever and Jackie are sisters-in-law, who have both settled down in Stratford. Here, things are hotting up. According to the papers, Perry is denying that he lost the country money in the 'tropical fish affair' and he has also denied that he has been seeking psychiatric help from a 'hitherto respectable practice'. But we were not mentioned by name.

Love Amelia

That didn't help me, of course. I felt that I needed to get back home to help Amelia but how could I leave, when Jackie and Ever might also need my help? I decided to stay put. After all, I hadn't yet resolved my issues about the *Macbeth* play, which intriguingly was yet to be written. The arrival of the King of Scotland in England had changed the atmosphere in the country, which now had also come out of a plague in which many had died.

We were well into the new year and there were all kinds of rumours about the Roman Catholics wishing to overthrow the new King. The irony was that Raleigh, a Protestant, was in the Tower for precisely that. Everything seemed to be topsy turvy as if the reversal of roles in *Twelfth Night* somehow had spilled over into society.

The Puritans, or Brownists as they were sometimes called, were objecting to the Catholic liturgical hold on power – but we are talking of the Anglo Catholics and not Roman Catholics. Roman Catholic extremists, however, were infiltrating the country and those caught and found guilty of sedition were being executed.

On 22nd February 1604, the King had ordered that all Roman Catholic clergy, Jesuits, Seminarians, and other priests were to leave the country by the 19th March. What had happened to the King's largesse? His promise of no discrimination? Would the priests leave the country, or would they stay and become martyrs for the sake of the truth – whatever that is? What was a Catholic? What was a Brownist? Who was loyal? Who were the traitors? I was thankful that Jackie and Ever were accepted as sisters-in-law and I laughed to myself about me having been thought of as a woman. Thank goodness I didn't dress as one for *Twelfth Night*. Even Spikey, when I mentioned it to him, seemed to think it was funny. He walked off shaking his back legs, but was this amazement or annoyance?

There was a knock at the door. Standing there was a man who announced that he had come on behalf of the Government to check my premises. He asked me where I was born, about my parents, who were obviously of different races, where I had lived until coming to London, and why I was there. I was well prepared and had documents from my previous visit to back up my story. He seemed satisfied with everything he read and he commented,

"So, you are mainly helping The King's Men in the training of actors, the evaluation of their talent and the nature of their plays?"

"Yes," I said.

"And what would you do," he continued, "if you considered one of the plays to be seditious and a danger to his Majesty and to the realm?"

"I would hope that wouldn't happen, but if it did, I would make my views known."

"And who would you tell?"

"I'd raise the issue formally with those in charge at the Globe or at Blackfriars Theatre."

"What if I told you that we hear they are considering putting on a play in which His Majesty is being represented?

I said that I hoped His Majesty would always be represented in a good light, reflecting the love and affection his people have for him."

"But to represent His Glorious Majesty on stage would be an offence. How would you make that clear?"

"I've never been in a position to do so," I replied, "Since I've not come across a play which has transgressed in that manner."

He thanked me courteously for my remarks and then changed the subject to the fact that I had apparently met His Majesty at Wilton House. He asked me what I was doing there and I told him that I was living in a cottage, thanks to the generosity of the Earl of Pembroke.

"And what were you doing in the cottage?" He asked. I answered that I was reading and studying books from the Earl's Library in the hope that one day I might be able to study at the University of Oxford.

"Have you ever been to Oxford?" he asked.

"Yes," I replied.

"Do you know the Salutation Tavern?"

"Yes, I know it and I have stayed there." He looked me up and down carefully. My heart was pounding. Thank goodness, I thought, that I hadn't shaved for a few days. He grunted and asked if I had something on which he could write. I showed him to my desk and he wrote something on a brand-new roll of paper that I had given him. He pocketed the message and the roll and then he turned and said,

"You were at The Elephant, the night that the host was attacked and one of the house servants murdered. I understand that you helped the host and that you covered up the servant girl who had been molested and killed. Whose clothes did you use to cover her body?"

"My wife's," I answered.

"Her name?"

"Ever Fortune," I replied.

"We hear that you acted honourably that night," he said adding, "You may like to know that those responsible for the woman's death have been apprehended and executed. I am entrusted to give you His Majesty's thanks. His Majesty is apparently interested in your work as a… "

"Psychotherapist."

"Ah, yes," he replied and smiled. "His Majesty would like you to stay in London in case he has need of you."

"I'd be honoured if I could be of service," I lied. He nodded and with that, he walked towards the door but turned and asked,

"Where is Ever your wife now?"

"In Stratford upon Avon with her sister-in-law Jackie." He nodded and left. I felt exhausted. After he had gone, I just collapsed in my chair and fell asleep.

I had a fitful dream in which the witches appeared to me again. This hadn't happened for some time, yet as before they whirled around me. I cried out for them to stop but they laughed repeating their earlier riddles;

"Beware if reflected fools appear."

"Sleeping brothers are dangerous."

"Turn three times to ward off foul consequences."

Were the riddles significant?

I woke with a start and panicked. I was troubled by my dreams – if that is what they were. Why did the witches appear to me? Were they warning me about being here in Jacobean London? Spikey, as if sensing my unease, came out from under the cupboard and jumped onto my lap.

"You're black aren't you Spikey?" I asked. He looked up at me. "But do the tabby and ginger cats discriminate against you? Back at home, 'black people' have been exploited for centuries, as have those of mixed race like me." Spikey settled down on my lap, as if in anticipation of a monologue. "The point is, Spikey," I continued, "In the age of this Scottish King, forceful independent women are in danger of being labelled as witches, and witches are regarded as women who have slept with Satan. Black people are of Satan's colour. Why did that man from the Government want to know about my parents? Is it that the King is fascinated with me because I am neither black nor white, but may nevertheless be associated with witches? What is it that Macbeth calls the 'weird sisters'? 'Secret, black and midnight hags.' We arrived at midnight, Spikey. You are black and I am of colour. We need to take care. We may be tolerated, but we are not one with them or with their King. But even in the 21st century, despite all the platitudes to the contrary, we are not totally accepted. So why should we expect anything but suspicion, here in the seventeenth century."

Clearly, Spikey was not too worried about any discrimination in the feline world as he had fallen asleep on my lap.

I was certainly being watched and investigated. I realised that even my notes were a danger to me but I needed them as a record of what I was experiencing. Half-awake half asleep I continued talking to my cat.

"Spikey, wake up!" I shouted. "Where should I hide my papers?" Bizarrely, the cat seemed to understand. He opened his eyes, jumped down off my lap and went under the cupboard. He then came out and mewed. I moved the cupboard to see that he had created an indented area for himself on the mat that I had previously placed there where he could lie down and yet look out into the room. I felt the floor beneath the mat and found there was a loose flagstone. I lifted it up and underneath was a space where something could be hidden. I collected my papers together.

"You wonderful cat!" I said, "Spikey, you are a marvel." He looked at me and watched me hide my papers. I then placed his cat mat back on the flagstone and he settled down on it. He seemed as happy as a cat could be in 17th century England, where it was unusual to have a cat inside one's premises.

CHAPTER 24

Anne Shakespeare had found work for Jackie and Ever. Jackie was to help with the silkworm business. Now that she was no longer male, she could not be seen as a doctor and her colour could have made it difficult for her to be accepted by the community unless she was a member of the serving class.

This problem did not exist for Ever, who at first, went back to being a seamstress working in New Place as part of a larger cottage industry, which Anne was developing.

Times were getting dangerous and people, who had disguised themselves for one purpose or another, were finding themselves in trouble. The plague was over and Jackie and Ever thought that maybe they should head back to London and from there back to their own century. Jackie, however, was as interested as I was, in how Shakespeare lived and worked.

It appeared that he had a personal library but when did he use it? What was Stratford like as a place to live when the poet, or at least his family, were there? He must have been commuting between London and Stratford regularly, although some historians had suggested that this was only once a year! What was his relationship with his wife? Were they still in love?

Anne spoke of him as if this were the case. There was a great deal to discover which I would enjoy hearing about when eventually we would all return to Amelia in the 21st century.

One day Jackie and Ever walked down to the river Avon and along the bank towards the church. They noticed a willow tree with many of its branches overhanging the water.

"Look at that," Ever said. "It's like the tree Ophelia climbs in *Hamlet* and falls to her death." They stopped to look at it. The place was very quiet and beautiful, with the river gently flowing along its course, but they were startled by a raven squawking. It was looking at them from another tree. As they looked around, an ethereal-like figure appeared from the direction of the churchyard. It was an old woman who approached and greeted them. She then stood in silence by the tree. They felt uncomfortable and went to move on but the woman held out her hand and touched Ever's arm telling her that this tree was the one that had killed her niece. Ever and Jackie stayed to hear the story. The old woman said that her niece had come to fetch some water and seeing the tree she decided to climb it. The branch broke plunging her to her death in the water below. It wasn't, she insisted, the fall that had killed her but it was that her clothes had wrapped around her and had become heavy, pulling her under the water.

"Oh, my goodness!" Ever exclaimed. "How awful. The same death befalls Ophelia in *Hamlet*." The woman was still distressed.

"How long ago did it happen?" Jackie asked.

"Over twenty years ago," the woman replied. "It was common knowledge about the town. Some, of course, asked why she had climbed the tree as it was so dangerous. But who could answer that? She just climbed it. It was as simple as that. It was a mistake and before help came, she'd drowned."

"What was her name?"

"Katherine Hamlett," the old lady replied, and with that, she went on her way. Ever and Jackie stood there stunned.

There had been a real tragedy but one incorporated later by a local writer into a play, using her surname. Perhaps it was just a coincidence.

As the two of them walked towards the churchyard, a black cat suddenly ran in front of them. They followed it until it stopped by a gravestone. It looked up at them as if to ask, "Was this what you were looking for?" The inscription read, *Hamnet Shakespeare 1596 aged 11.* To lose a child is such a tragedy for any family, whatever the century. So much history is frozen, so much is lost in time – a future denied. A voice called out 'Malkin' and the cat walked off towards the old lady, who was now sitting by the wall of the graveyard. Jackie and Ever made their way back to New Place, not so much sad as thoughtful.

When they arrived, Anne Shakespeare was in conversation with her friend Judith Sadler, who with her husband ran a new bakery, their old one having burnt down. Jackie and Ever were treated to some buns that Judith had brought over. Ever told her that she would like to try baking some cakes. Judith looked puzzled, so Ever described the sort of decorated cakes that she would like to bake. Judith was fascinated and said Ever could try out some recipes. Ever realised that she would not have access to all the ingredients she used in the 21st century but thought it would be good to experiment. The next day Ever went to the bakery. Her cakes worked out so well that Judith offered Ever work there. After some trial and error, Ever produced some intricate pastries which sold well, as the bakery's fame spread through the town and county.

CHAPTER 25

I had been back a good few weeks when an anxious Augustine appeared at my consulting room door. He seemed to be a little panicked.

"Has anybody been here to see you?" he asked as he pushed into the room and sat down. "Several people," I replied. "Business has been looking up since I arrived back from Wilton. But I imagine that you have concerns about the man who came from the Government"

"What!" he exclaimed. "You mean from Cecil? He is the government! A man has been here from Cecil?"

"I think so, although he seemed more interested in me having met with the King."

"Oh, that makes it certain that he was from Cecil." Augustine sat back in his chair. "They want to know who you are. They'll have found out about the King's accident and his visit to the cottage."

"Visits!" I said to myself but I decided not to make things more stressful for Augustine.

"We were worried about your sister having impersonated you but it seems that wasn't the reason for Cecil's man being here."

"No, it wasn't, but I realise now that you know all about my twin sister. I can assure you that she is safe in Stratford with Ever and that she is no longer impersonating me. Everybody is happy that they are sisters-in-law." I refrained from saying 'lovers' as that would have given him a heart attack!

"We've been so worried about you," Augustine said, "especially since you came back from Wilton, but actually before that. During the time when the Queen went ill, there were lots of rumours about you being a woman. Then Will saw you at Oxford when he knew that you were at Wilton. But he had worked it out already. He'd have heard the suspicions because of his plays about cross-dressing. He is into all of that from a comic point of view of course. Between you and me I think he makes a little too much of it but don't say anything to him. He gets upset if I criticise him! So, this man from Cecil just asked you about being at Wilton?"

I answered, "More or less. Also, he wanted to know about my work with the company and what I'd do if I found out that subversive plays were being planned."

"Really?" Augustine started to get a little worried again. "And what did you say?"

"I told him that I'd seen no evidence of anything subversive and that if I did, I would report it to the management of the theatre."

"You mean to me?" Augustine said, sitting forward in his chair.

"No, I mean the shareholders."

"Well, that includes me and means me. The others don't do much of the business work, not since Burbage Senior died."

Augustine relaxed back but became thoughtful. "Jacob," he started and then hesitated. "Jacob," he began again, "Did anything happen when the King met you that you haven't told us about?"

"Of course not. I think he was just interested in me and the science I espoused. That's all. The official was satisfied with all that I had said, and then he left." Augustine nodded. I felt I'd said more than enough.

"Be careful Jacob," Augustine warned. "After all, the King has a strange reputation! Did you know that we've decided that to flatter him we are going to perform the Gowrie play."

"What!" I exclaimed.

"I know you, Pembroke and now Will have qualms about it but the writers and the cast are really keen to go ahead with it. They believe that the King will enjoy it because he comes out as a hero."

"Don't you know that even his wife, the Queen has doubts about what happened with the Earl of Gowrie and later with his sons? It is a dangerous subject."

"Well, the players with few exceptions, think otherwise. We've sent a copy to the Stationers' Register and we are going to give a first performance tomorrow at Blackfriars Theatre."

"What about Shakespeare's alternative play *Macbeth*?"

"We are leaving that idea on the shelf for a while at least. So, it has been decided we are doing the Gowrie play." He smiled. I said that if that was the company's decision, I hoped it wouldn't turn around to bite them. He laughed and invited me to attend the performance the next afternoon, which I did. There was a reasonable audience and the play started quite well, with the Gowrie brothers deciding that they'd have to see the King about a financial matter for his benefit. Then in the next scene, as Richard Burbage playing the King walked on, armed officers suddenly burst into the theatre and mounted the stage. The play was stopped and the audience was sent home. Burbage and the cast were interviewed and it was decided that Augustine, Burbage and John Heminges (another actor) would have to report to the Master of the Revels to whom they were immediately taken.

I sighed and came back to the consulting room where Will was waiting for me.

"I warned them," he said, "They can't say that it was bad luck."

"Perhaps it may be time for *Macbeth*."

"What do you mean?" he asked quizzically.

"Your Scottish play and bad luck!" I said, "They go hand in hand, not one before the other."

"You are quoting from my *Comedy of Errors*," he laughed. To which I replied,

"Yes, certainly it isn't in *Macbeth*." He looked puzzled and took his leave, but as he left, I could hear him muttering to himself, 'Why not *Macbeth*?' I just need to write it."

CHAPTER 26

Following the February 1604 order by the King's Government that all Jesuits and priests of the Old Faith must leave the country, there was a further crackdown on the Catholics. This, ironically, heightened their activity, especially in the Midlands, where there had always been an unease about the breach with Rome. Clopton House, not far from the town of Stratford, seemed to be a centre of discontent and was raided regularly but the authorities were disappointed. There were no priests to be found only a bunch of 'cobblers and scribblers'.

Jackie was getting on well with Anne Shakespeare and was finding out a great deal more about her than she was about Will. Much of the income of the family seemed to come from the lucrative silkworm business which Anne was running from New Place. Some of the silk was sold locally but more went to London and on to the costume makers for the theatre, including Mountjoy's in Silver Street where Will now had lodgings.

One evening, Jackie helped Anne to find some books which Will needed in London. Going to the library, which was on the upper floor, was a wonderful experience. It was filled with papers, books, illustrations, quills etc. It had a large desk on which there were old scripts and new books. There were quarto editions of plays on the shelves and the floor and there were scrolls some of which were in good condition whilst others were dog-eared. It was a crowded chamber of books and manuscripts – so many that she couldn't take it all in. She looked around and her mind went into a spin. It seemed the room was turning itself, as titles and names flashed by her eyes. They were circling her, script after script.

Whilst they were looking for the particular books, Jackie heard a familiar voice downstairs. She thought it might be Will, but it turned out to be Edmund his younger brother, who'd come to collect some books and take them to Will in London. Anne came downstairs with them. Edmund greeted her, took the books and was off in an instant. He seemed to be a young man in a hurry.

Jackie and Ever were still very much in love with one another. When they had to resort to being sisters-in-law rather than husband and wife, Jackie had given Ever a simple ring. It was the only sign of their relationship. Ever wore it on her right hand but took it off while baking. One afternoon she realised that she had left the ring in the bakery. Although she could have gone back the following morning, she was adamant that she wanted it immediately, so she went back to the bakery for it. She found the ring easily enough but realised she wasn't alone. She could hear voices in the back room. Why would anyone want to be there at that time of day? One voice was louder than the others and was speaking a language she did not recognise. She gently nudged the backroom door open. She saw the Sadlers in prayer with some other local people and to her astonishment Shakespeare's daughter Susanna, Michael Drayton and Ben Jonson. Two other men were at a table at the far end of the room, which was ecclesiastically dressed like an altar. One of the men was serving the other with some wine. She recognised him as Nicholas Owen, whom she had seen in

Oxford. The other man, dressed in a chasuble, had his back to her. A Roman Catholic Mass was taking place, strictly against the laws of the land. She wasn't sure what to do but as she moved away, Susanna saw her and put her finger to her lips.

Ever knew what it was like to be a dissident. After all, in the 21st century, she was a non-binary person, refusing any pronouns whether male or female. In those days Ever had dressed in the most extravagant clothes and had suffered lots of insults. Why should others suffer, irrespective of what they believe? Ever had no belief in God and saw the Mass like other religious ceremonies, as a ritual needed by some to help them through life. If people wanted to believe, why shouldn't they? If they wanted to believe in an old rite, why not allow them to do so?

There were no secrets between Ever and Jackie and the two discussed the issue later that night. Ever explained what she had seen. Jackie's first concern was for Susanna whom they had grown to know whilst living in New Place. She felt that Susanna needed to be assured that her secret and that of the back room at the bakery, would remain as such. Since the Scottish King had come to the throne, the religious tensions, despite all his promises to the contrary, had risen exponentially. Recusants, who refused to join the Church of England, were in more fear now than in the days of Elizabeth. At least, the former Monarch had tried to take a line of toleration for the Old Faith. But that hadn't worked. The Pope's excommunication of her had led to the influx of Jesuit priests, inciting those of the Old Faith to rebel or even assassinate her.

"What is religion about?" asked Ever in exasperation.

"It is about love for one another," Jackie replied. "But for those who run Church or State or Church *and* State, religion is about the exercise of power – ultimate power – not just to make judgments on earth but supposedly in the afterlife."

"It's all nonsense," Ever said, with disgust.

"Maybe it is, but for those who believe, it brings the peace and consolation that life is not worthless. It is only in extremes that it is flawed. Too often it results in people killing or having been killed because of disagreements about the nature and rules of the religion itself."

"But look at the problems it causes with people's mental health. We, as psychotherapists, know the problems caused by trying to hold two opposing views at the same time. Forcing people to hold one set of beliefs while they actually have a different set, leads to psychological tensions. It is a cruelty from above."

Jackie and Ever knew that the new Pope would formally excommunicate the Scottish King for his continued adherence to the English Church. It seemed a fresh cycle of doctrinal rebellion and revenge had started. If there were a God, he must have been crying on his cross.

Having agreed that they needed to assure Susanna that nothing would be said, Jackie and Ever met with her the next day. She looked as if she had been awake most of the night. They went for a walk through the Mulberry Garden and told her simply not to worry. She said that she wasn't so much worried about herself, people knew she was of the Old Faith, but she was concerned about her friends, the poet Drayton and the dramatist Ben Jonson who had been there. Susanna explained that Jonson had been staying with Drayton nearby and they had come together. She thought that perhaps her father shouldn't be told about the visit. Ever and Jackie assured her that her secret was safe and if it were to come out, it would be hundreds of years later when they were all dead and gone. Susanna looked puzzled.

Issues were building up so much for the Catholics that even Susanna would have to conform. For now, Jackie and Ever just advised her to take care. They knew what it felt like to have to be vigilant when not conforming to expectations, whether religious or social. Susanna however, had a maturity about her to know not to fight when the battle is lost. That Sunday she accompanied her mother when she went to the parish church, where she took communion, as did the Sadlers. Even Jackie decided that she should conform and attend the Sunday service, although it caused a bit of a stir in the church because of her colour. Ever made it known that she was there, but defiantly remained in the porch.

JOURNAL

Freedom is a right. If people are confined in mind and body over issues of religion or through tyranny, they will eventually rebel. Amelia had told me of the atrocities that had occurred in Israel and the horrific retaliation in Gaza. People on both sides of the border were being slaughtered or displaced because of long-standing religious disagreements, conflicts and tensions. It seemed that an eye for an eye, a tooth for a tooth, and blood for blood had become the order of the day, even in the 21st century.

But in the early seventeenth century, I realised that in breaking with Rome, Henry VIII set in motion, a reign of terror between religious groups. There was widespread discrimination, where people were treated differently, according to their religious persuasion. It was to lead to civil war, two decades after Shakespeare's death, but the problems would continue for centuries to come. The dictates of one man had put in motion the misery of others yet to be born.

CHAPTER 27

Peregrine was desperate to keep himself in the public eye. Having decided to 'spend more time with his family' and lie low for a while, he had done the exact opposite. He had inveigled himself onto a cheap television show, ironically called 'Roulette'. It resulted in him being on the front page of *The Sun* newspaper, placing his bets in a fish tank full of water with the heading 'Chips and Fish'. But now he didn't mind the satire. It was all publicity, which was what he craved, thinking that 'all publicity was good publicity'.

He was even seen photobombing a television news interview with one of the Finance Ministers outside the entrance of Downing Street. He had walked past the interviewer, noticed what was happening and then immediately returned, walking past again, grinning closely to the camera.

"What a plonker!" Dafydd said, but Amelia explained that it was a symptom of self-obsession, and attention-seeking, possibly stemming from childhood. He needed to be seen, even if he was ridiculed in the gutter press or people laughed at him on the television and in the media.

Helena Rousseau, the acerbic probing journalist, who had

destroyed far bigger fish than him, was planning to interview him on television. He was keen to go onto the programme as he believed he had nothing to fear. He thought that if he could just tell the truth and the way he had sorted out the issues relating to the illegal sale of tropical fish, he would be believed. He thought that there was no more to be said.

But there was plenty to be said. The Chairman of the Party and a few Members of the Cabinet were worried, not about Peregrine but about themselves. The 'fool' Peregrine could cause trouble for them if he were to be interrogated by Helena. Some members of the ruling party had made vast amounts of money, as had many of their friends in the ingeniously complex tropical fish scam, which had disguised their financial wheeler dealings. They were concerned about what secrets might be exposed. It was important to get Peregrine out of London and into an isolated place, away from the attention of the media. They knew that he would not willingly leave the British Isles. Also, he wouldn't resign from Parliament without a strong incentive to do so.

The new Prime Minister (the third in two years) had been a Member of the Cabinet, who had benefitted from the 'tropical fish arrangement' and some insider dealings involving the Russians. Now he and the Party Chairman, who had served all three Prime Ministers, discussed the problem over cognacs in their London Club.

"Could we make him a business advisor to Fiji?" asked the P.M.

"That wouldn't attract him as he doesn't like rugby or the heat. But Peregrine has always wanted to be a Lord – a title that he has dreamed of since childhood. Yet we could not possibly give him a place in the House of Lords. Too many questions would be asked. Rousseau would be even more eager to get Peregrine in front of the camera, precisely because she knows that the issue is far deeper than him.

Then the Chairman suggested, "You know there are still places in the far north, in Scotland, where Lordships can be bought, attached to a piece of land. Maybe we could give him one of those where he could happily use the title of 'Lord' even though he would not be a member of the House of Lords."

"Do you think he would settle for that?" asked the P.M.

"Well, if he believed that the alternative was a prosecution for money laundering, insider dealing and corruption, he might well think it was a good offer."

"Can you arrange it?"

"We have some donors in the Caribbean who would like to ensure that he is silenced, but I think that they would be willing to finance the purchase of the land and title for him."

The P.M. agreed that it was a better solution than the one offered by another advisor, who recommended an accidental fall from the top of Blackpool Tower after tempting him with an offer to go on *Strictly Come Dancing*. That, after all, could damage the programme which was rather popular with the viewers and could make him more of a household name.

The Chairman also had contacts in Moscow and Sicily who could deal with the matter, but it was decided, that a Lordship in the north of Scotland plus a good pension from the House of Commons would suffice.

Peregrine was made the offer. At first, he was reluctant but finally saw the sense of accepting it, although he wasn't sure how he would convince Camilla.

He turned up at *4 Psychotherapists 4 U* with the news that he had finally been made a Lord and from now on he would be called Lord Barnes of Ronaldsay. He exclaimed that he and Lady Barnes were excited to be going to live in Scotland, in an area which he thought was not too far from the Monarch's residence at Balmoral, where they were sure that one day they would be invited to lunch or even for Hogmanay.

With that, he took his leave of Amelia and the Practice.

Amelia reported the whole story to me, explaining that she

didn't charge Peregrine for his last visit, since it was of no consequence. Helena Rousseau was given an interview with the Prime Minister who in answer to her questions merely repeated them back to her, in a different linguistic order. The government ploughed on towards the next election.

CHAPTER 28

I n 1605, the authorities in London were clamping down on any kind of disruption to the social order of the new political regime, including any theatre where satire reared its head. It wasn't only Will and Augustine who were having problems with their plays. But it seemed to me that two years of rule by the Scottish King had resulted in a greater fracturing of society than I'd seen in my earlier visit to the London of Queen Elizabeth 1. There was a sense of unease with the influence of the Scots at court and the new religious restrictions.

In March, Will had gone to stay with the Davenants but was now back. On his return to London, he said, "I wanted to be in Oxford for the birth of my son," before quickly correcting himself, and saying, "for the birth, that is, of my godson, William." A slip of the tongue no doubt! He was very proud of his godson, whom he said would do great things in the theatre once he was of age.

Wherever the playwright Ben Jonson had been during the winter, by spring of 1605, he was also back in London, where he had teamed up with dramatists Chapman and Marston to write a new play, *Eastward Ho!* It looked as if Marston had made his peace with his fiery colleague after the earlier quarrel.

Jonson had something of a temper and had once killed an actor over a disagreement. In court, he claimed the 'benefit of the clergy'. This was a simple test of being able to read out and translate a passage from the Bible. If you could do this, it proved you were a learned man and therefore should not be executed. You could only make this claim once and if it was judged to pardon you, you were branded on your thumb so that if you murdered anyone else, you couldn't be granted another stay of execution. Perhaps that is why, in his quarrel with Marston, Jonson claimed that he only cudgelled the young satirist who had made fun of him on stage. The theatre gossip was that a contrite Marston had dedicated his play *The Malcontent* to Jonson. I suggested to Augustine that perhaps Jonson didn't understand its implications in the name of the play and he should be careful because Marston had retained a 'malcontented' grudge.

Marston, Chapman and Jonson had agreed to work on the play *Eastward Ho!* The story was developed and the roles were written individually for each actor. The roles were given out and the date of the performance, when the three poets were to meet again, was set. They were anxious to see how the comic play would be received. I was concerned that the play wouldn't be so much comic as dangerously satirical. I was right.

Jonson and Chapman met at the Blackfriars Theatre for the first performance but Marston didn't turn up. He had left London and rumour had it that he had gone to Norwich, a town becoming known for recalcitrant actors and poets. At first, the play went well with the audience. They were enjoying the humour but much of the comedy depended on ridiculing Scottish accents. It was judged to have gone too far, however, when it ridiculed a Scottish character, who closely resembled the Scottish counsellor to the King and who had responsibility for the Monarch's 'natural needs'! Sir John Murray, the 'Groom of the Stool', was furious and had the play stopped, in full flow as it were. The bewildered Chapman and outraged Jonson were arrested and taken to the Tower. They claimed to have known nothing of this particular scene. I deduced that it must have been scripted by the absent Marston. It was the young man's sweet revenge on Jonson! The two 'innocent' dramatists were imprisoned with threats of their ears being sliced off and their noses split as if they were common prostitutes. Augustine later told me that Jonson's mother, despairing of such indignity for her son, had brought a vial of poison for him to take, should the necessity arise and she claimed that she would also take some herself.

On the evening after the disrupted performance of *Eastward Ho!* Augustine and I met for drinks at Wilkins Tavern.

"It could be all up for Chapman and Jonson," Augustine said. "Chapman is so learned and Jonson writes such good plays but they've taken a step too far with this one. It just shows you how careful you have to be. Cecil knows everything. He probably knows that I'm talking to you now."

"Did they write the pointedly offensive lines?" I asked.

"I don't know," Augustine shrugged. "Marston was involved and knowing him, he probably was getting his own back on Jonson, whom he considers to be conceited and pompous. Gossip has it that he has been sent for by Cecil or Coke or someone on their behalf. It seems all a little shady. Some people are saying that the papists are to blame."

I asked whether Jonson, as rumoured, was a papist.

"He might be, or he might not be," Augustine replied. "Maybe he's in the pay of Cecil, watching us, watching them and characterising them on stage. On the other hand, maybe Marston has sold his soul to Cecil. Both he and Jonson walk a fine line between what they do and what they say. Chapman, however, has true friends around the King and perhaps they'll get him off."

It was the talk of the theatre for the next few days. Will somehow learned that one of the letters sent from prison was to Esmé Stuart, the son of one of the King's 'closest friends', the late Esmé Stuart, Duke of Lennox. Another of the letters seeking help went to Pembroke and one from Chapman, he understood, 'went to the King directly'. We later learned that Marston had been brought back and severely reprimanded on behalf of the King. He was strongly advised that Mary Wilkes, the King's Chaplain's daughter would be a fitting wife for him and that 'he might consider being a spokesman for God rather than a satirical commentator on the court.' His satire was getting to a point where he could lose his head and entrails. Marston's days of writing satire seemed to be coming to an end.

Much to Augustine's astonishment, Marston did marry Mary Wilkes in the King's chapel. Whether or not the King demanded his 'droit de seigneur' – the right to be in the marriage bed, which he was prone to do when agreeing to marriages at court – we could not discover. But certainly, the King's appetite for sexual adventures was being widely discussed around the theatres and elsewhere in London.

I didn't hear much of Marston after that episode but in a sense, he had been protected for one reason or another. Jonson and Chapman were released with ears and noses intact. I realised that maybe I was an innocent among spies. Jonson continued writing as if nothing had happened, but as Marston had prophesied at Wilton House, Jonson renounced his Catholicism.

After Amelia had read my latest report, she wrote to me.

Dear Jacob

Your mention of Will's slip of the tongue about his godson, William Davenant, raised my curiosity. In his later life, Davenant did claim that Will was not only his godfather but his natural father. Maybe that is why he was christened William?

Love Amelia.

I replied,

Dear Amelia,

I don't believe that story. I have discovered that it is usual practice for the godparents to give their names to their godchildren, as happened for example with Will's own twins, Hamnet and Judith. They were named after Hamnet and Judith Sadler. I reckon that William Davenant liked to mention Will as being his natural father as it somehow exalted him. This was unnecessary really as he was reported to be a brave man, who continued to perform plays during Oliver Cromwell's Commonwealth, when the Puritans banned theatres and performances altogether. Maybe Davenant was just joking. I am sure that Will made a genuine slip of the tongue.

All my love,

Jacob.

CHAPTER 29

I n November 1605, all the talk was about the Government nearly being blown sky-high by the Great Gunpowder Plot. The traitors in the plot were rounded up. Some were killed in skirmishes. The rest were brutally hanged and dismembered in the glory of the King's name. There was much anxiety about it all. The King proclaimed that Catholics in general needn't be afraid as only those associated with the plot were being hunted down and arrested. Was that true or was the plot being used as an excuse to get rid of any 'enemies of the state'?

During all this turmoil, I kept a low profile. It was dangerous to be an 'alien'. I kept to The Elephant and my consulting room. Augustine came round to see me daily with all the news. He told me that Jonson had known some of the traitors. He'd even been seen drinking with them but apparently although questioned he wasn't detained. Was he ever a Catholic? I wondered because he had professed to be so in public. Or was Jonson, as with dramatists in the past – most notably Marlowe – actually a spy, reporting on what was being said at the theatre and around the city? Augustine and I noted that he certainly was being exalted by the court and was involved in and developing the lavish masques that the Queen loved so much and in which she performed. Indeed, he was making more money with his engagements for a single masque than he could possibly make writing his plays for a whole year. I could see him as a rising star with his claims of Catholicism being well forgotten.

When things quietened down a bit, in early 1606, Will and I started to meet regularly at Wilkins Tavern. At one of these drinking sessions, Will told me that Jonson had been engaged to write *The Masque of Blackness* for the Queen and her ladies to act out at court. It was part of a political expedient in trying to get the King to restore a religious service in which the Monarch, by just touching an ill person could restore their health. It was something King Edward the Confessor was rumoured to have been able to do. Will explained, "It is all nonsense but Jonson was paid a fortune to devise *The Masque of Blackness* for the Queen, in which she and her courtiers blackened their faces. The Masque made out that the power of the King's touch, would eventually, turn them white! So, Jonson is now expecting another commission, which will be the sequel called *The Masque of Beauty*, when the women will all appear again, having turned a beautiful white. It is grotesque, obscene! How could Jonson be involved himself with such an offensive idea?"

"Money?" I suggested, "And patronage of course."

"Sycophancy more like," he replied, "But you are right about the money. The rumour is that there was a budget for the first masque of £3000. It is a fortune. I can't be involved in that kind of extravaganza." He then said sadly, "None of the court came to see my *Othello*, which I hope was a sympathetic portrayal of a black man, tricked by a white man, into murder."

To cheer him up I told him that I'd played the role in a rehearsal at Wilton, which made him laugh. I also told him that the play would be performed for centuries. He hoped that was true. I continued, "I am writing a journal about my time in

Jacobean London and what is happening here. It seems that the number of executions are increasing. People are too easily being linked with last November's atrocities."

"Yes," said Will. "Did you know that a Jesuit, Nicholas Owen was horrifically tortured and then, after confirming that he had constructed the priest holes where Jesuits could hide, he was publicly executed? He was a wreck of a man even by the time he arrived for the execution." He continued, "One of his Jesuit friends, Henry Garnet, was hunted down until he was found in one of the priest holes stinking of excrement. When being questioned at his trial, he had pleaded equivocation."

"I believe the Jesuits, in particular, make an art of equivocation," I added.

"In Garnet's case, it was to no avail and he was executed. Some of his followers ran onto the gallows whilst he was noosed and hung onto his legs so that he wouldn't suffer evisceration while he was still alive. Of course, the executioner still went ahead with the disembowelling and quartering afterwards, just for the crowd's entertainment."

Will continued, "These are times in which the lie has been turned into the truth and vice versa. It is an age of equivocation and it comes from the highest source." He took another drink from his tankard, looked around the room to ensure there was no one who could hear us and he whispered,

"The King is a liar and a hypocrite. He sleeps with attractive young men while having others executed for doing the same thing. How can he do that?"

I smiled. "By force," I said wryly. But told him that even one of his boy actors had asked me the same question.

"I bet that was Augustine's young lad, Alfred."

"You are right," I replied.

"He is a good lad and I have him in mind for the main female role in my next play. But coming back to my question, how can someone condemn people to death for doing the same things that they are doing?"

"Psychologically," I replied, "It can be a means of coping with a side of life that the perpetrator does not understand. It's like a purgation of guilt that he has for something which in some people is natural to their very being."

"I don't like him," Will emphasised, "He is a hypocrite. But in your time is homosexuality open and free?"

I told him that in some countries it was.

"How wonderful that must be," he replied, looking into his tankard.

"I admitted that in my time there were many who still did not tolerate it, but I believed that love is important. All you need is love," I said, "and if our love wants someone of our own sex, what right has anyone to condemn it?"

"It's personal," he replied. "You live your life as your heart and soul suggests."

"Of course, and by my reading some of your poems I think you have experienced it."

"Jacob, you are a wonder," he responded with a laugh. "You talk about poems which you could not have read." Despite the effects of the drink, I saw my opportunity. I knew I could ask the question that haunted me.

"Tell me, who is Mr W.H.?"

"Mr W.H.?" he replied. "What do you mean?"

"You dedicated your sonnets to Mr W.H. and people have been arguing about who that might be."

"Have they?" he asked.

"Yes," I said excitedly adding, "So who is Mr W.H.?" He looked at me with a beam on his face, saying,

"I've not written a dedication to my sonnets, as they have not yet been published, Jacob, but Mr W.H.? That's an enigma. What a joke! Thank you for giving me the idea."

I was crestfallen. He left the Tavern, muttering "Mr W.H., what a good idea, no one will ever know." He laughed to himself, "But they'll argue about it for years to come." He even stopped in his tracks to chuckle as I watched him going towards the theatre. He almost had a skip in his legs as he went on his way. At least the concept of Mr W.H. had relieved him of some of the tensions that he had. I must admit that I was tempted by the Tavern owner, George Wilkins, to have the pleasure of one of his 'girls' but I resisted and made my drunken way back to The Elephant where I collapsed into my bed.

CHAPTER 30

Following the gunpowder plot and well into the new year of 1606, the country was febrile about the religious divisions in the kingdom. The plot was an audacious attempt to bring about regime change. I thought that it was strange that despite all the spies, Cecil had only discovered the plot a few days before the planned assassination attempt – or had he known earlier and had played a waiting game? One of my clients, Henry, happened to be in the service of Cecil. He was quite open about his position in the 'treasury' but I suspected that he had come to me for 'mind help' as my clients called it, to find out about me and perhaps about the Globe, with which I did so much work. He was probably just following on from the official who had visited me before. I did not doubt that I had nothing to hide but I felt uncomfortable whenever he came to the door.

The 'game' he used as a means of trying to trap me was to give me little bits of information or put to me nonchalant questions such as whether I had been to the execution of Henry Garnet.

"No," I replied, "but I gather he equivocated himself to the gallows."

Henry laughed and changed the subject, saying that if we weren't vigilant there would be other attempts to murder the King.

"One of the trials and tribulations of leadership," I commented, "is that some will be opposed to you. The more important you are, the more vulnerable." He agreed and then talked about his own private issues in relation to marital matters which need not concern us here.

One morning, I had the feeling that someone had been in the consulting room again. I asked Spikey if he had been disturbed in the night. I shooed him away from his mat under the cupboard and checked under the flagstone. Nothing had been disturbed. Maybe Spikey had frightened off whoever it was. Perhaps I was being paranoid.

Interestingly, earlier that March, there was a rumour about an attempted assassination of the King near the town of Woking. There had been a cry of 'treachery', with someone fleeing through the crowds. Rumour quickly spread that the King had been murdered. Somehow from there, it continued to spread like wildfire across the country. It was then announced, to huge rejoicing, that the King was alive and was returning to London. Crowds came out to see him but I remained in my consulting room.

I talked to Will, who had called round for a drink of my 'famous tea' to which a few of my clients had taken. "Were you not frightened for the King's life?" I asked.

"Rumour," Will replied. "Just rumour." And with that, he quoted himself:

"Open your ears, for which of you will stop / The vent of hearing when loud Rumour speaks?"

I laughed, "So what do you think it was all about, Will?"

"It was about Power and Glory. The King needs to consolidate his power, does he not, after all that has happened?

"So," I interrupted, "the strategy might have been to create a false rumour about his supposed assassination to continue to ensure that there was popular support for him, even after the gunpowder plot."

"Exactly." Will said. "People need to be given a link to Power through those wielding it. They fear for the powerful figure as a reflection of their own insecurity. If the powerful man can demonstrate that he can overcome the odds, then they will have faith in him. So why not create a false rumour that he is dead and then allow him to reappear in good health?"

"I agreed. Psychologically people in positions of authority like to feed on their notoriety, drawing attention to themselves to consolidate their positions."

Will smiled. "Likewise, our Scottish King is enveloped in a lavish display of love wherever he goes, especially after the false rumours of his death, and further so-called assassination attempts. Maybe the Woking event was all planned that way from the start, a clear subterfuge on the government's part. Or maybe they just capitalised on a minor incident, enlarging it into something important."

"Precisely," I concurred but added, "Alternatively, this King could just be paranoid, thinking that there is opposition to everything he is doing, or trying to do. But you can understand this paranoia since some headstrong Catholics did try to blow him up!"

Will smiled and then went thoughtful before saying, "Jacob, as I've told you before, I don't like this Monarch. He is fickle, unreliable, hypocritical and untruthful. The late Queen Elizabeth, whom I liked, had many problems with him about money. She provided him with grants to prevent the Scots from threatening England by making pacts with France or Spain. However, he squandered the money and came back for more and more. After the Queen's death, it was better for Cecil to get him on the throne than to have the threats continue into the next reign, especially if Cecil could remain in power as Lord Treasurer. The King will say anything that makes him look good at the time and then he will go back on his word or even worse deny it when times change, or different problems arise. He always looks for the easy life and the easy lie. The issue with the Catholics is a case in point. He promised toleration but continued to fine them until he was ruining them financially. He then brought in this new Oath of Allegiance, supposedly to help them, but which actually ties them up in the way it is written. It does not give them the freedoms he promised. It was because of a frustration about freedom and conscience that they wanted to kill him. You rightly imply that he may have constructed a means to spread false rumours about other attempts on his life. There is no truth in the man. He is a habitual liar and yet I have to write a play supposedly to exalt him." Will sat back in his chair and frowned.

"Supposedly! But you are not going to do that are you?" I asked.

"Absolutely not Jacob. I'm going to do the opposite. I'm going to write a play which seems to glorify him, but which reveals him to be nothing but an evil shadow, cast across our land and for that matter of Scotland." He then reminded me that Henry Garnet, the Jesuit priest who had been executed, had been indicted for equivocation, using words with double meanings to hide the truth. Will said that he was writing a play on equivocation, which if you looked behind the superficial image, you would see something deeper.

"This is the play called *Macbeth*?"

"Yes," he said. "I'll make the Scottish King think himself to be the heir of a kingdom steeped in glory but in reality, it is steeped in deceit and bloodshed. He will think that he is a descendent of Banquo, father of Kings, but look deeper and he will be shown merely as a pawn of history, signifying nothing."

"Do you want me to help? "I asked eagerly.

"I do," he said, "I want you to help my actors take on a story which draws out an equivocating narrative, so they can appreciate the uncertainties in the characters and the plot. They may come up with ideas which are contrary to what my writing on the surface may at first imply. Their interpretation needs to appreciate the equivocal."

"I am sure that they will complain that a play means what it says not what it doesn't say."

"You are right," Will answered. "This is why they need to make up stories for themselves."

"And the best story," I proposed, "Is one that they create or defend themselves while in character. It is important therefore that when they come to see me, they are in character so that I can hone it appropriately."

"Yes. I will have done enough," he said, "in writing the play. It is your job to get the players to see behind the façade, look into their own psyches and create their own histories as characters, finding ways to fine-tune the roles they play. That is what I presume a psychotherapist is all about." He grinned at me. He was a mischievous character as I had found out once before. "Remember, Jacob, they are who they are. I have created these characters not just for this play for my time but also for the future. The meaning will change depending on those who are acting it."

I took a deep breath.

"I understand about your Scottish King as I do about our authorities back home in my country. We have had our fair share of deceit, hypocrisy and habitual lying – the times and circumstances might change but there is an evil strain in politics which focuses not on the people but on the politicians."

"Exactly," he said, "But for now let's have some Mad Dog." I sighed as Mad Dog was the strongest of ales and therefore, I knew we were in for another long night's drinking session at Wilkins Tavern and a rotten headache the next morning.

JOURNAL

The incident with the supposed assassination of the King reminded me of something that happened in the 21st century. The COVID pandemic struck and many people started to die from it. There was fear about the spread of the disease and lockdowns as happens when plagues strike. During all of this, there was a strange phenomenon. The leaders of certain countries and others in government announced that they had contracted the disease and had to be taken to hospital. The spokespeople for the leaders gave regular medical announcements about them, even to the point that the population were told that their leader had nearly died. Would you believe it, they all came through. They were said to have suffered just as the people had suffered. They had fought off the disease and were leading the nation again. Maybe it was true that the leaders had contracted COVID and perhaps that in itself had given people hope. But maybe it was exaggerated as a part of a political manoeuvre to consolidate the leadership thus exploiting a real emergency amongst the people for the politicians' own egotistical purposes. With politicians, how can you tell what is truth and what isn't?

Shakespeare was on to something in writing *Macbeth*, which is often thought of as being about overreaching ambition. Maybe there is far more to it than that and if so, what will the hypocritical Scottish King make of it?

PART II
MACBETH

CHAPTER 31

Y ou think you are in charge, that your mind has a grip on what you want to do and as a psychotherapist, you need to have that confidence. The mind still plays tricks. I still don't know whether what happened was true or delusional. A few days after talking to Will, I returned from my lodgings to find the three weird women in my consulting room. Spikey was under the cupboard, out of sight. I assumed he was deliberately keeping clear of everyone. One woman was sitting on the floor and the other two were in the consulting room chairs. They were scrawny, dishevelled and somewhat frightening.

"What is it that you want?" I asked.

"Peace out of fear," one said.

"Stability from instability," said the second.

"Truth from lies," said the third. I told them that I didn't understand but they said in unison,

"Of course, you understand, otherwise you wouldn't have spoken." Then they were gone.

It was bizarre. Was I daydreaming? Had they been there or were they just in my mind as I thought of the task that Will had asked me to undertake? There should be no mystery in all of this. When you watch a play, you believe in it. If you see *Macbeth* being performed, you believe in the three weird sisters. The witches came and the witches went, just as in the play, but were they telling me to be true in the world that I was experiencing? I wondered if there was electrical interference which was blurring my vision. Spikey crept out from under the cupboard, looked around and purred, raising his tail as he came towards me. He seemed to be quite happy but maybe that was because I gave him some food. I asked him if he had seen the witches, but he just ignored me and continued eating.

It was the following day that Macbeth arrived. He reminded me of the Scotsman that I'd seen at Wilton House and earlier at my consulting room. However, he didn't wear a kilt but was dressed in a brown woollen tunic. He had a presence about him, a confidence that he was aware of what he was doing.

"Have we met before?" I asked as I invited him to sit down.

"No, I don't think so."

"You have come to talk to me?" I took my seat opposite him.

"Why else would I be here?" He looked around my room. "It's a rather strange place. Do you sleep with the cat?" He asked as he watched Spikey sauntering back towards the cupboard.

"No, the cat sleeps here but I have rooms elsewhere."

"Really," he replied and sniffed. He was not regal like Hamlet had been but rather down to earth. He seemed to be aspiring to authority rather than having it, like a Home Secretary who would like to be a Prime Minister but lacked the talent. I felt that I had to make a conscious effort to be professional towards him. What I needed to explore was why he acted as he did in killing King Duncan. The simple answer, of course, was his desire for the crown and certainly that was there, but were there other factors and other issues going on in his mind? What had the witches said to me? 'Peace out of fear, stability from instability, truth from lies'? Did they correspond to the riddles they had given me earlier?

"I didn't have to come to see you,", he said, "Indeed I think it is a waste of time, but I am my own man and I come of my own volition. You may be able to make sense of what has been happening to me."

For me, this was a useful opening. In saying he was his own man, and that things had been happening to him, he was trying to portray himself as a victim. But instead of being the victim, he was the aggressor. So, what was this inversion all about? I made it clear that I was there to listen to him to contextualise his situation.

"What does that mean?" Macbeth asked sarcastically. "Contextualise my situation? You educated doctors think you can confuse me with your language. Let's make it clear, I am the King, the legitimate King but some scoundrels want to usurp me, dethrone me, and even kill me. These traitors say that Malcolm, the son of Duncan, is the true King." He leaned forward jabbing his finger at me to make his point. "By law, I am the anointed and crowned King of Scotland. Of that, there is no doubt. It was attested as such by the Thanes at Scone, the sacred place where our kings are acclaimed." He raised his voice, "I was confirmed as King and once acclaimed, anointed and crowned, no one can dethrone me except God himself."

He was now so sure of himself that I thought he was going to finish the sentence with 'except God himself if he dared,' but he didn't quite go that far. This was a determined man, younger than I thought he would be. My first impression was incorrect. He had an authority but perhaps with a brutal, bullying side.

"So, what is worrying you?" I asked. There was a silence. He fiddled with a ring on his finger and looked away towards the window and the street.

"What can you possibly do for me?" he said. "You are a mere doctor of some kind."

"I wonder," I replied," If you'd like to tell me why you killed your predecessor. No lies, just tell me the truth." He fell silent as did I waiting for him to respond. At last, he began,

"It is true I did kill my predecessor". He then paused and said," I wanted to banish fear, to bring an age of peace and stability. That is what I wanted and felt required to do. So, yes, I killed my predecessor." He paused and then went on to say that he had killed old King Duncan – not that he was all that old. "Duncan, King of Scotland, the great hypocrite of our times who some were now calling a martyr and a saint." He looked at me as if I didn't understand. He continued, "Can you believe it?" he said in disgust. "Let me tell you about this saintly Duncan. It was all a façade. He was a weak, miserly, manipulative, vow breaker. I was loyal to him. Macdonald revolted, so I killed Macdonald, opening up the traitor's belly till his guts fell out onto the ground before he fell and rolled into them. Macdonald wasn't a bad man. He was my friend. I killed him because he had gone too far and openly rebelled against King Duncan. He wanted freedom from the irksome tyranny of the supposed religious old King. You know, the most effective tyrants are those who don't, on the surface, appear to be so." Macbeth leaned towards me again. I didn't say anything and I tried to show no emotion. He pointed his finger at me.

"Duncan played at being old." Macbeth paused. "Too old to fight." He paused again. "Too old to remember that he promised me the crown so that I would fight for him. Perhaps he had once promised the crown to Macdonald. I don't know. Do you see?" He looked at me angrily. "But I do know that I was to be King Duncan's successor. I bet the stories about me don't say that, do they? Before the battle, the old hypocrite told me that I was his favourite. His sons were no warriors. They didn't have it in them to fight. Duncan told me that Scotland needed a warrior king. So, he said, that when he died, I was to be the one he had chosen. I went to battle with the Norwegians and I killed them and the traitors like Macdonald. But no sooner had I done that…" He paused, got up from his chair and started pacing the room. I said nothing. He continued, "I came back from battle, victorious, expecting to be confirmed as the next King. Can you credit it, Duncan proclaimed his cowardly, ineffectual, spoilt son Malcolm as his successor. What had Malcolm done? Had he been in battle? No. He'd be on the verges of the battle, a voyeur, merely a looker-on. Had he been wounded in battle? No. Neither had his cowardly little brother Donalbain. I couldn't believe what I had heard. How could I let Duncan get away with that? Somehow the witches knew what was going to happen. I met them when I was with Banquo and they told us. They made it clear, however, that I would find a way to be King. They must have known that a promise had been made and that a King's promise was sacred. It was my duty to ensure that the promise was to become reality. I believe that the old hags were observers, not instigators, as some people say. No, I am my own man."

He came back to his chair and sat down. He fixed his eyes on mine. I remained silent. He continued, "Before agreeing to fight on Duncan's behalf I had told my wife about his promise. I could have revolted with Macdonald. I could have served him as King and I know that Macdonald would have made me his successor as he had no children. I was a fool. Macdonald would have kept his word. But I had made my choice as I had already got a promise from Duncan. My wife was suspicious of Duncan and as it turns out rightly so but she was also wary of Macdonald. She thought he was an unsavoury character and she didn't like him. She agreed, somewhat reluctantly, that I should fight for Duncan. Against all the odds I fought my way through the soldiers and I reached Macdonald, whose offers I had rejected in favour of Duncan and I…"

I noticed that he gritted his teeth and shook his head again as he thought about the way he had killed Macdonald.

"I killed him without mercy or blessing, the man I should have served. But it was Duncan who waited for my victory and then reneged on his promise. In front of many people, he praised my valour and this duplicitous King then ignored me announcing that Malcolm would be his successor. It was all political. I was a victim of political ambition and I had been outmanoeuvred. I could do nothing about it. Now people say that I was the ambitious one. But how, after all the praise he'd given me in winning the battle, could I call him out as a filthy liar? I couldn't shout at him like a little child and say 'That's not fair, you promised the crown to me'. And then the worst of it was, what was I going to tell my wife? I'd fallen into a political trap and I feared that she would think of me as a failure, a loser." He paused in his tirade. I remained silent as clearly more was to come but he turned it into a question. "What do people say about Duncan? What will history say about him? You tell me."

"It's not for me to say," I replied.

He shrugged and continued, "Well, I'll tell you. They will say he was a saintly King, like Saint Edward the Confessor of England. A man surrounded by candles and incense, who could heal the sick by the touch of his hand. And do you know what I'll say to them? I'll tell you!" He stood up again and walked to the window. As he turned around, I could see his eyes were burning with emotion. "I'll tell you," he repeated. "Candles and incense are for the dead. I killed the hypocrite for God to take care of him. Duncan was not worthy to be on the Earth, only under it. They'll say Macdonald was a traitor and that Macbeth was a traitor. But I say that the hypocrite, Duncan, was a traitor to his people."

Macbeth sat down again and leaning towards me he continued, "None of the people who tell this history will ask why we were fighting the Norwegians in the first place. But I'll tell you that as well. Duncan had flattered Norway, borrowed money from them and now they wanted it back. He'd made promises of trade and then he directed that trade to Denmark. He could renege on promises he had made by donating money here or there. The Norwegians were furious. They had lost patience and had come for what was owed. Macdonald knew about it as he was the one who told me. But of course, the invasion was made out to be unprovoked. It was not! The irony was that our soldiers were now being financed by the loans that the Norwegians had given us. They were fighting against the soldiers that they had paid for. Our soldiers! Can you believe that! Originally the money was meant to finance our invasion of England but according to Duncan, it didn't matter whom we were at war with. He kept himself miles away from the conflict. Macdonald had had enough of Duncan's duplicity and hypocrisy and so had I. That is why I determined to kill Duncan when he reneged on his promise to me. Of course, the official story, which is told, is the one put about by Malcolm and Donalbain. They said that their father was unjustly and brutally murdered for no other reason than my ambition. But the truth, the real truth, is that Duncan was a money-grabbing thief and a traitor to his own people and let me tell you, a sexual predator. He deserved to die and I was chosen by the Agents of Justice to kill him."

"The Agents of Justice?" I asked incredulously. "Who are they?"

"Never you mind." Macbeth retorted. "I've had enough of this today. You have awoken a lot of emotional turmoil in me." He got up and went to the door. He said, "I will come back again but this has been too much. Your silence has unsettled me. Just think about what I have said."

To pacify him I replied,

"Yes, I will."

JOURNAL

I had hardly probed at all but frankly, what he had said made sense. I'd heard the story in other contexts. Why does one nation invade another? What promises are made? Hadn't I been told recently that the King of Scotland played Elizabeth off to gain money by pretending to ally with France or Spain until she paid up? Maybe Duncan, not Banquo, was an ancestor of the Scottish King? What is the truth when in my own time an invasion of another land can be called a 'military operation'? Is it all to do with the way the leader controls and frames the narrative? Language is undermined.

There again, what is truth? Not so long ago my own country invaded another, looking for 'weapons of mass destruction', which they never found. The whole region was destabilised. But now when another country invades its neighbour, calling it a military operation, it is condemned, probably rightly so, but what hypocrites all these political leaders are. The interest is in themselves and their authority and control. It's not in those who are slaughtered or who grieve.

CHAPTER 32

Macbeth's wife, without an appointment, turned up at my door the next day. She introduced herself and said that she wished to discuss certain issues. I agreed and suggested she could come the following day. "No, I want to see you now." With that, she pushed past me into the consulting room. Fortunately, no one else was with me except Spikey. She took one seat and I took the other. Spikey jumped up onto my lap and stared at her.

"Don't you know that cats should be outside not inside? They are infested with all sorts of diseases and fleas," she said. Spikey looked offended by her remark, jumped down, swished his tail and went under the cupboard, where he was able to look out and growl softly at her.

"This is an inside cat," I answered, "He wears a flea collar and I prefer cats to rats and mice." She thought for a while and smiled. It wasn't the answer she'd expected. I'm sure she didn't understand what a flea collar was, but ignoring the remark she started,

"I have heard that you are gathering information about my husband. So, let me tell you that he is a good man."

"I'm sure you think he is," I replied, "But people come to

see me about themselves, not about others, even those close to them. That is what psychotherapy is about, a one-to-one interaction between client and psychotherapist."

"Well," she said, "My husband and I are as one."

Curt language was already revealing her character. She was direct and confident with at least a touch of arrogance. I said that I understood the relationship between a husband and wife, but I wanted to know what I could do for her. She said that she needed to talk to someone because she and her husband had not been understood and there were all kinds of accusations about them.

"What kind of accusations?

"That we are incredibly ambitious."

"And are you?"

"No, we are not."

"Tell me a bit about yourself and let's get back to ambition later," I suggested. From what she then told me, I deduced a terrible loneliness and fear in her. Every time her husband left the castle, she did not know whether he would return. In his absence, she was frightened that the castle would be raided or that she would be attacked. She had no children to worry about but that increased her fear of isolation whilst he was away. I inquired if she had ever had children. She said that she had given birth to a child when she was married to someone else.

"So, you've been married before?"

"Yes," she replied. "To a Thane who was killed in a battle fighting for his country."

"When was that?"

"Years ago, the last time the Norwegians invaded."

"And who was King of Scotland at the time?"

"Duncan, of course," she replied. "He has been on the throne all my adult life." I made a mental note of what she'd said as this was something quite new to me.

"And your child?" I asked.

"Andrew."

"What happened?"

She looked at me with sad eyes. "My late husband killed him whilst teaching him to fight."

I'm not often surprised but this did take me back. "Would you like to tell me about it?"

She sighed and began, "Andrew wasn't strong, but he liked stories, especially about great warriors. He imagined himself to be one. My husband naturally felt Andrew needed to be toughened up and trained, so he started to train him in warfare. I didn't wish it to happen. I liked Andrew as he was – a lively little boy, innocent, and not at all competitive. But once the training began, a competition started between father and son. The boy did well and my husband egged him on, building up his skills and confidence. But one day, my husband thrust, Andrew parried and my husband instinctively thrust again. Andrew did not move quickly enough. He was wounded and three days later he died. My husband had forgotten to place the guard over the blade.

The doctor said that Andrew had lost too much blood inside his body. My husband could not forgive himself." Lady Macbeth sighed deeply and wiped away her tears as she relived the painful memories. "Before long there was a skirmish with invaders from Norway. My husband was involved in the fighting. Macbeth told me that a Norwegian sword was thrust towards my husband, but he did not parry. Instead, he dropped his sword to the ground. The Norwegian ran him through and then took off his head. That's all there is to say about it. Having seen what had happened, Macbeth killed the Norwegian and brought my husband's head home from the battlefield. We buried it in my son's grave – the two of them together. Sometime later Macbeth asked me to marry him and I consented, but I insisted that we had no children, not unless he became King and put a stop to our wars. That was an agreement between us. With all my heart, I wished for peace."

I thought this through and asked whom she blamed for her son's death.

"Why, Duncan King of Scotland," she replied.

"And what about your husband's death?"

"Also, Duncan King of Scotland," she said abruptly.

"And why is that?" She explained that Duncan was a manipulator who used people for his own means. He had continued to take the country to war in which many had been slaughtered but he and his family rarely went to the actual battlefields. They stayed far away, praying for victory! I asked that if this was the case then why did people continue to fight for him? She replied that it was like a disease. Duncan could raise competition among the Thanes, pitching one against the other, each vying to be better than the others and sustain the most kills. To be a man you needed to take wounds, inflict them and kill. To Duncan, war was like hunting, although this too he liked to watch at a distance. Who would kill the most aggressive stag? Who would risk his life in the hazard of a hunt? It was never King Duncan because he always found an excuse to watch rather than to participate. The Thanes were proud and he played on their pride and their competition as well as his own constructed saintliness. But the time arrived to take revenge on behalf of those he had killed. He had to die just as they had died, except that he was in his bed when the blade struck whilst his sycophants of the chamber around him were drunk out of their minds."

"Do you mean," I asked, "That those who were drunk were not just guards but rather Gentlemen of the Bedchamber?"

"Of course," she replied.

"So," I asked, "who was the one who killed him?"

"Why, my husband, of course. Macbeth is a professional killer. He kills for King and country. His task was to kill for the country because the King was unworthy of leading anymore. I believed that once he had killed the old hypocrite, we would have peace in honour of my son, who was sacrificed for war.

This is what he did. But Macbeth is a good man. He is the opposite of Duncan, who played at being the saint. Macbeth has his faults but also his virtues. The greatest of these is his regard for others. That is why he had to be King. It was a virtuous, heroic act."

"And when did this happen?"

"As soon as he returned from battle. I understood that King Duncan was coming to honour us with a visit. So, I said to Macbeth, that this would be Duncan's last night on earth if I had anything to do with it. I couldn't wait for the next day to come."

JOURNAL

Lady Macbeth certainly was ambitious but the back story she gave was one of expiation and revenge as well as one of hope for a rule of justice and peace. She chose not to understand how solutions can bring unforeseen problems. She hadn't understood the implications of the realpolitik. This was the opposite of the story usually told, the overlying story of the Shakespearean play, written to please a King. In her version, Lady Macbeth and her husband were manipulated victims of a divine King's selfish and fickle exercise of monarchical authority. Which was the true story? The backstory as Shakespeare had asked me to encourage, struck me as one which put everything out of focus. It distorted the facts that we were normally given. This was just like the way the facts of the Gowrie fiasco had been distorted. Which Gowrie narrative was the true one? The one told by the King or the one favoured by the Scottish Kirk? In the first narrative, the King was exalted, in the second he was the assassin. In the story of Macbeth, was Duncan, a saintly victim or was he justifiably removed because of his hypocrisy and misrule? Lady Macbeth was forcing me to look through a distorted mirror rather than at the reflection of events with which I was familiar. The alternative to the received interpretation, as she saw it, provided a narrative that was diametrically opposite from my own, and from that of others who were familiar with the play. Where was the truth? Which narrative would prevail?

Was it my job to challenge her? I don't think so. The deed was already done. She left expressing that she would return in due course. But she begged me to be kind to her husband as he'd done no harm. He hadn't murdered Duncan but merely executed him for the expiation of his war crimes.

Lady Macbeth's revelations made it abundantly clear that a backstory to their performances could give further insights. Yet I'm not sure that she told the whole story. At times she hesitated as if there was more to say. She also wanted me to be kind to her husband. Why wouldn't I be? I'm a 'mind doctor', not a jailer or executioner. Perhaps there is more for her to say or reveal. I will have to have patience.

CHAPTER 33

Perhaps Will was thinking of the Scottish King while writing his portrayal of Duncan – saintly on the outside but rotten to the core inside. Perhaps Duncan was one of those Kings, who when he visited a castle, felt it his duty to have his way with the lady of the house, if not the man. Could the character in the play be interpreted that way?

Lady Macbeth hears that the King is arriving and she says, "The Raven himself is hoarse / That croaks the fatal entrance of Duncan / Under my battlements." Why hoarse? Is he not just calling for death, but reminding her that Duncan has been here before?

Duncan, in contrast, calls the place 'a castle with a pleasant air sweetly welcoming.' He and Banquo talk not of ravens but of 'temple haunting martlets.'

Who was kidding whom in this visit by Duncan, the raven or the martlet? What did King Duncan want in coming to Macbeth's castle? Thinking about it, what had the Scottish King wanted in going to Gowrie's castle? Visits of Kings were always dangerous one way or another, financially, sexually or mortally.

There was no doubt in my mind that Macbeth was a

murderer and that he was assisted by his wife, even prompted by her, but was this just about ambition? Might there have been more to it than that? And what had Will told me about the play? He was having to write a play to honour the Scottish King, who had already shown himself to be rather bored by Will's work. I was mulling over this issue when there was a knocking at my door.

"Who's there in th' other Devil's name?" I asked myself as I opened the door and found Macbeth and Lady Macbeth standing outside.

"We've come," Macbeth said.

"Just as you suggested." Lady Macbeth added.

"Together," continued Macbeth, as they walked past me into the room.

It was true. I had mentioned to them that I might like to see them together, although, of course, I had seen them individually first. They decided that it was time for both of them to arrive and who was I to turn them away? My approach would be different from seeing them as individuals as I needed to observe their interaction, which I would probably do by asking questions, rather than just listening. They made themselves comfortable in my consulting chairs, one in the brown leather chair for clients and one in mine. I decided to sit on top of the desk. Spikey came out and strolled around, looking suspiciously at the two of them.

"Why do you still have a cat in your consulting room?" Lady Macbeth asked. "Cats are not supposed to be inside. They should live outside."

"As I told you before, not this one," I said. At that Spikey gave a withering look towards the intruders in his domain and he flicked his tail at them before disdainfully disappearing under the cupboard.

Macbeth reminded me that I had suggested that they might come to see me together. I realised that this couldn't be a psychotherapy session, but an inquisition in which I would have to question the two of them.

I said to them that it seemed to me that they had both participated in a single irreversible act which one of them had actually committed 'off stage' as it were, whilst the other, having encouraged it, stressed about whether it had resolved a difficult situation or not. I said I wanted to play a game with them as Christians, which I assumed they were. They agreed but asked what game.

"I'd like you to think of me as the doorkeeper, not to hell as in a play that might be written about you, but to heaven. I want to question you about the assassination."

Macbeth, at that point, stopped me saying, "'Execution' not 'assassination.'"

I apologised and continued, "About the 'execution' of King Duncan." My aim was to get an idea as to how the murder came about. I started therefore by asking Lady Macbeth what she thought when she received the message that her husband was coming back home, after having defeated the Norwegians.

"Well, of course, I was happy and relieved," she immediately said. "It was far better news than I had received that awful day when I was told of my first husband's death, serving King Duncan." She looked at me as if I'd asked a stupid question. I noticed, nodded that I understood and asked her to relive the moment in detail. She told me that one of the servants had come to her with great news.

"And what great news was that?" I asked.

"Not only that my Lord was coming home to me, but that King Duncan was coming to stay."

"Were you pleased that Duncan was coming?"

"I thought of death, Duncan's death, that had to occur with Macbeth's arrival."

"Go on," I said.

"I can't. Far too deep, too private." She shook her head and then gave me a hard stare.

"I understand but if you really wish to know, even to exonerate yourself, which is why you have come to see me, you need to say a little more." I recognised that the conversation by this time was becoming something of a dance between the two of us.

"But my husband is with me now, he wasn't then," she replied.

"So," I said, "Are there secrets between you? Cast your mind back to that moment and to what you wanted." Lady Macbeth swallowed hard, looking at me and then at her husband. I prompted further, "What did you feel and how did you express it?"

"I wanted my husband," she said. "No one else." She paused and Macbeth smiled at her. She continued, "I felt a determination, no I felt a deep desire within myself so that I called on the agencies of darkness to take the softness of my sex from me and make me one instrument from head to toe, determined on a single act – the execution of Duncan. I wished only that in myself, in my blood and flesh to have no other feeling than my total determination that nothing should come between my purpose and me." Macbeth looked at her and like me, he noted that she was single-minded as she said. "I called to the spirits to come to my breasts and turn the issue of love into the poison of death."

"What do you mean?" I asked.

"The milk from my breasts no longer needed to be something that attracted men and fed life but now would rather end it." She replied. "It was something not to be seen but hidden in the darkness of the dead of night when there could be no light, no escape but only the blade of my dagger, which would free us from the tyranny and sin of the so-called saintly King Duncan."

She sat back in her chair, almost in relief. I understood what she was implying. This wasn't just a killing out of ambition. It was a woman who perhaps had been humiliated. It was revenge. Macbeth looked at her with bewilderment. Did she carry a secret between Duncan and herself?

I went on to ask Macbeth, "How did you go about actually murdering the King? Can you describe for me and for your wife how you perceive what happened?"

Macbeth confessed, "Well, I told a servant to get my wife to ring a bell when my drink was ready."

"What drink was that?" I asked. Macbeth shuffled.

"Any drink," he said irritably, "It was just a signal that all was ready for me to do the deed."

"What happened then?" I asked him

"I saw a dagger hovering in the air."

"A dagger?"

"Yes."

I sat forward on the desk and looked hard at Macbeth, asking him to tell me about this dagger.

"It was horizontal, its handle towards me, the blade pointing to the place I wished to go."

"What did you do?"

"I tried to hold it, to clutch it but somehow it wasn't there. It was as if it wasn't real and yet I could see it."

"And how did you feel inside?"

"I felt it was something in my mind, my desire, but it still looked so real. I pulled my own dagger from its sheath but still, this dagger of my mind remained, directing me to where I needed to go and what I needed to do. Nothing else mattered. I entered Duncan's bedroom and coldly thrust my dagger, my real dagger, into him time and time again. His eyes opened, of course, but he didn't struggle much. His life was soon extinguished. I staggered back to meet my wife, the dagger dripping blood onto my hands. The dagger was covered in blood, death's blood. I could hardly stand the sight of what I had done. I cried out that this hadn't happened. But it had happened and it was right that it was so."

Macbeth looked at his wife, and continued, "I could see the

blood before my eyes as if this dagger had cut through the innocence of sleep."

"And...?" I asked.

"All the evils of the invisible world were around me, celebrating as if in a ritual chant of murder, murder, murder. They had encouraged me to do the deed, to make the imagined, actual and now they were celebrating that it was done. But what kind of man did that make of me? "

Macbeth stopped and looked at his wife again. She was crying, not just at what he had said but at what she may have recalled. I had touched a hugely sensitive area.

"Sit back both of you and relax." I offered them some water which they both accepted. "Thank you," I said, "for explaining to me what happened and why it happened. I am not Peter at the Gate of Heaven if such a place exists, but I understand that this 'execution', as you call it, came about from something far more sinister than ambition. But for today that is more than enough. You have delved into your minds and brought your thoughts into the open. We will meet again but probably individually next time."

I noticed that Lady Macbeth held her husband's hand as they left my room and I thought,

"These two are in love but will it continue?"

JOURNAL

In order to provide a backstory, which gives a justification for Lady Macbeth's behaviour, she used the accusation that Duncan was a lecher and she a victim. This was a reasonable enough proposition, since over the centuries, Kings and Princes have had a tendency towards lechery. Even today women and indeed some men, are playthings to provide a consolidation of individual power through sexual dominance. I remembered a saying that 'truth is so hard to tell, it sometimes needs fiction to make it plausible'.

CHAPTER 34

My darling Jacob

I have been reading your notes. I want you to know that I have worries about you and need you to take care since you are multitasking in your own Jacobean existence. Remember you are a psychotherapist whose function is to help people understand their motivations and their actions. In this, you have expertise in the 21st century. But you have now re-entered the 17th century and are having to make judgments about people living within that cultural environment, not your own. Furthermore, when dealing with *Macbeth*, you are entering a fiction, based on stories related to a historical figure going back to the 11th century and appearing in various myths since that time. This must be putting a huge drain on your personal and psychological resources. Take care of your own mental health.

All my love, Amelia.

Dear Amelia,

I understand all that you say and your concern about me. I'm entering the psyche of the characters I describe, but not in the way of literary critics or indeed historians. I am looking at them as psychological entities, being depicted and recreated by actors, who are themselves human beings. So much is often prompted by what we know historically, theatrically and by the fiction of the people living again in the actors that portray them. I'm teasing out for Macbeth, and more particularly Lady Macbeth, deep issues which are not said in words but may be the undiscovered motives of their actions. Duncan was the King of Scotland. There was a tradition amongst royalty to demand sexual favours from those whom they ruled. It is something which, as you know, even goes on in the present day – and not just with royalty but with other 'authority' figures. It seems that throughout history, such people can live by one code, whilst demanding that those they govern, live by another. They surround themselves with mythical qualities, to justify both their authority and their conduct. I wonder if this might have been the case with King Duncan, who possibly created the myth of sainthood surrounding himself – or did others do it for him?

I am aware of the dangers but as you know the mind of a murderer is complex. We know from 17th century history that the Danish-born Queen of Scotland had furious tantrums possibly brought about by her husband's monarchical culture. These could have played a part in at least two of her miscarriages. In the play Lady Macbeth talks of herself as being capable of plucking her nipple from the boneless gums of a baby and dashing its brains out, if she had promised her husband that she would do so. For those determined Royals, one real and one fictional, the life of a child was immaterial. To me, that was an awful realisation.

But is it just ambition that makes Lady Macbeth so cruel? Could it not be frustration, as in the case of the Danish-born Queen's treatment by her husband? Could it be humiliation as with those women who suffered royal traditions such as the 'droit de seigneur' – that of a royal visitor in the middle of the night?

Aren't there contemporary parallels with males today, employing their positions of power to exploit women and men on whom they have forced themselves, sexually and / or mentally? Under the guise of historical fiction, the theatre explores such abuse and obscenity: 'The play's the thing, wherein I'll catch the conscience of the king.'

One thing I have found out in being here in the early 17th century is that I am not so far away from you in the 21st century. Do not worry, I will persist with the quest.

Your lonely, but loving husband,

Jacob.

CHAPTER 35

There was a knocking at my door.

"Come in," I cried. It was Augustine who seemed somewhat anxious. "We've had confirmation," he said, "That the Queen's brother is coming from Denmark to visit the King."

"That means the King of Denmark is coming to visit the King of Scotland and England again," I replied.

"Oh Jacob, don't be so pedantic, not today. Everything is going wrong."

"Well, it certainly caused problems the last time the King of Denmark came, since by all accounts the two Kings regularly got drunk out of their minds at Theobalds. Cecil was furious, as was the Queen, who has been complaining about his drinking."

"Jacob," Augustine retorted, "you are not supposed to know anything about that. You sometimes say too much."

"Or too little." I replied, "But let me make some tea and then we can talk about it."

Augustine really did seem to be in something of a state. He sat down and then he got up again, walked to the window and looked out.

"Another body in the street," he said.

"The carters should pick it up before long. It often happens. Sick people make it up to this street from the river, where they've probably drunk the mucky water and they die here. I had one die right outside the window some days ago. It quite distressed me. I just saw somebody keel over and by the time I had run out of the door and up the alley and round to him, he was dead. Maybe I should have jumped out of the window in the first place to help him."

"He'd have died anyway," Augustine said solemnly as I gave him his tea. I had distracted him with a diversionary tactic I often use. The story of the man dying by the window could have been true and Augustine believed it, so it had served its purpose.

"Will is furious," he said.

"Why?"

"This play he is proposing to perform for the King is a tragedy, which isn't something the King particularly likes. But at least I understand it has witches in it. We thought therefore that we could liven it up a bit."

"Liven it up?" I asked. "What do you mean?"

"Well, knowing the King has a hatred for witches, we thought we could do something with them."

"Like what?"

"Well, for example, we could have them fall into a vat of boiling oil, as happened in one of Marlowe's plays. But, of course, that's been done already. Or, as one of our dramatists Cyril Tourneur suggested, we could have them accidentally kill themselves whilst trying to execute someone else. Thomas Middleton is all up for something like that but he has also suggested that we should have them singing and dancing, you know, around a cauldron and even around the auditorium. We could make them fly. It would make it much more entertaining and less serious if you know what I mean."

"Let me tell you…" I started to say. But there was another knocking at the door.

"Come in, in th' other the Devil's name," I called.

"Who are you calling a devil?" Augustine said with a laugh.

"Just quoting Will," I said, as the man himself burst in and said to Augustine,

"I thought you'd be here – getting to our psychotherapist first."

I saw that Augustine was ready to go into verbal conflict with the dramatist.

"Hold it!" I said. "Sit down Will and have a cup of tea. Remember you can only get this tea with me so please don't quarrel with each other while I make your drinks." They sat staring at one another at first and then Augustine looked to the window and Will to the door in silence. As I handed him his cup, Will said to me,

"Jacob, you know *Macbeth* is a serious play, a tragedy. The words are clear, the structure defined and the story laid out. We have a tragedy, a genre for which I am famed, ready to be performed before the King."

Augustine went to reply but Will then added something which wasn't quite true in my view, "Before you say anything, Augustine, it has nothing to do with the Gowrie play that got you into trouble." Augustine jumped up and went over to the window again, on the pretext of seeing if the carters had picked up the corpse. I stated that *Macbeth* was at least an alternative.

"Exactly," Will said, "And it appears to be politically neutral."

"Well," I continued sceptically, "it is about the murder of a King, which I'm not sure can be seen as 'politically neutral'."

"The murder of a King of Scotland!" Augustine exclaimed, "How can we have a King of Scotland murdered on stage in front of a King of Scotland and a King of Denmark? He'll be asking to revive *Hamlet* next, where the heir to the throne goes mad and, in the end, all the Danish Royals lie dead on the stage."

"Most of the deaths in *Macbeth* do not happen on stage.

That is the nature of tragedy, they happen off stage." Will replied.

"So, King Macbeth isn't murdered on stage?"

"No, he isn't murdered on stage. Also, King Duncan is murdered off stage." This perplexed Augustine a little. "So, what happens to King Macbeth?"

"At the end of the play, he is killed off stage and his bloody head is brought on to the stage to present to the new King."

"What! Not to our new King?"

"No, no," Will said. "No, the new King of Scotland in the play, who is Malcolm." Augustine tried to get this all clear in his mind.

He said: "One: there is the murder of a King of Scotland named Duncan.

Two: at the end, there is the death of another King of Scotland named Macbeth.

Three: Macbeth's head is then presented to the new King of Scotland whose name is Malcolm."

Everyone agreed. Then Augustine asked, "But why is Malcolm made King?"

"Because he is the son of the murdered King Duncan, who had said, near the start of the play, that his son Malcolm should be King," explained Will.

"So," Augustine continued, "you intend to stage a play before the King of Scotland and the King of Denmark without any musical entertainment, in which two Kings of Scotland die off stage. The one being murdered by the other and the murderer being slain by... who kills him?"

"Oh," Will said, "That is one of the other Thanes of Scotland, named Macduff, because King Macbeth has not only slain King Duncan, but he has also slaughtered Macduff's wife and children."

"The King of Scotland has done what?" Augustine exclaimed, "He's had the wife and children of a Scottish Thane all slaughtered?"

"Almost all done in the best possible taste, off stage," Will quickly interjected.

"And is that it?" Augustine asked in astonishment, adding "As far as the murders go?"

"No, no," Will said. "He has also had another Thane, Banquo, murdered."

"Why?"

"Because the witches foretell that Banquo will be the father of the Kings of Scotland."

"And who exactly is Banquo?" Augustine asked.

"He is Macbeth's best friend," Will answered.

"King Macbeth murdered his best friend who is the ancestor of our Kings?" Augustine asked incredulously.

"Yes. It shows our Scottish King that he is Banquo's heir."

"At least that's something!" Augustine thoughtfully conceded.

Then, I said something which I shouldn't have said, but I had to show off, which really isn't in my nature.

"The irony is that Banquo never existed."

"What?" said Will. "Of course, he existed, he is In the Holinshed's book on the History of the Kings of Scotland!"

"I know that," I replied, "Holinshed probably thought he existed but actually in an earlier History of Scotland, Hector Boece made up the name to give our current King's late forebearers a dynastic heritage."

Augustine and Will appeared to be thunderstruck, expressing how disgraceful it was for historians to make up facts that simply were not true.

"But you do it too, Will," I said. "You made Hotspur the same age as Prince Hal in *Henry IV*, when he was Henry's father's generation."

"That is different," Will replied, "I write historical fiction, to entertain an audience. I don't have to keep to the facts."

I pointed out that he was also changing history with his mirror in *Macbeth*.

Augustine shouted, "What mirror?"

I explained that in the play, the witches conjure up a succession of Kings from Banquo, finally bringing on a mirror, which reflects them as a multiplicity of Kings into the future, presently culminating in the reflection of our current glorious King of England and Scotland."

Will suddenly joined in and emphasised,

"You see if the current Scottish King is present in the audience, the mirror doesn't have to reflect the procession of the Kings, but we could turn it to reflect him as the current heir of Banquo!"

Augustine, now excited, said, "Hell's teeth! That is brilliant. It's an idea sent by God. It is so good that I'll tell Middleton that he can forget about introducing lots of songs and dances, although he might still write a speech for Hecate, the goddess of the witches... and one song?"

Before Will could object, I interrupted, saying that it would be a good compromise. "Because Will, Hecate's name is mentioned at the start of the play."

"Well, that is true, but..." Will said.

Before he could finish, I interjected, "Excellent, then, that is all agreed."

Augustine immediately concurred. "The King will love it as the mirror focuses directly on him, making him the centre of attention in the play. Music beforehand, with singing and no doubt dancing, would totally destroy that effect. The mirror episode will also please the King in front of his brother-in-law, the King of Denmark, assuring him of who is in charge of England and Scotland as the successor of a line of historic Scottish Kings."

"And all the Gowrie stuff will be forgotten and forgiven," I said, winking at Will, behind Augustine's back.

"Assuredly," stated Will.

Augustine was pleased and added, "We can pacify

Middleton by promising him that he can stage a play about witches entirely on his own, at a later date."

"Don't give him too much to brag about." Will said, "But in principle, I agree."

So it was that a crisis was averted.

Augustine left my room, but I signalled that I wanted Will to remain.

I needed to talk to him about the stratagem with the mirror and whether it simply flattered the King, which is what he didn't want to do.

"Of course, it does, on the surface," he said. "So, I have a line from Macbeth's character saying 'horrible sight' as the mirror is turned towards the King. In reality, however, it is a truth but the Scottish King, seeing himself, won't realise the fact from the fiction. He might not even hear Macbeth's words! Underneath as we know and the cast will know, it is farcical, since as we have just said, we are aware that Banquo never existed. That makes it even more appropriate. What we must not do, however, is make the proud Scottish King look like the intemperate fool that he is."

I agreed, adding, "In time to come, everyone would know from history what the truth was."

"Maybe," Will replied. "I hope so, but can we trust history?"

With that, Will went to leave the room but I stopped him saying,

"Will, did you already know that Banquo was a fictional character?" He smiled and said,

"I asked my young brother Edmund to go to my library to check. He brought back a copy of Boece's *History of the Scottish People* where it makes it clear that there was no such man." He winked and left, presumably to go to the theatre or possibly, Wilkins Tavern.

CHAPTER 36

L ady Macbeth came to see me a day later. She went straight to the leather chair and sat back, ready for business. I decided to continue in questioning mode.

"At your last visit with me, when you came with your husband, he said that after killing King Duncan, he was asking himself if he had lost something in trying to gain the crown. How did you feel? "

"I was elated. At last, my husband had been the man I wanted him to be. I'd drugged the guards and the Gentleman of the Bedchamber so that they were asleep. I made it look as if they had been drunk, pouring wine around them and then taking some myself. I felt elated but on edge. I imagined my husband thrusting his dagger into Duncan's body, that evil, exploitative, so-called divine King. I was worried, of course, just in case it had all gone wrong, but it hadn't. This is what we'd wanted. Duncan was dead. Macbeth had been born to be King and I'd helped him to achieve his destiny. No more now, would I worry about the battlefield or about Duncan's visits to our castle. No more sleepless nights wondering if my husband were dead or alive, whilst I remained vulnerable. My husband was now King and I love him more than I can say. I'd been in the room and gloated over the dead body. It hadn't been so difficult to snuff him out. When I realised this, I knew I could have done it myself. I hadn't. It was not my role to kill him. It was my husband's and he had done it. I felt satisfied but he was anxious when he came to realise that he'd forgotten to smear the drunken guards with Duncan's blood. So, I returned to do that and do you know, I luxuriated in it. The evil filthy dishonest King was no more. I peered closely at him. I can see him now."

"Was there no remorse?"

"This was both a bedroom and a battlefield, don't you understand? It was a place of masculine victory where I could rejoice in my husband's love for me. Macbeth was my King. I closed my eyes and drank it up, the achievement, that glorious atmosphere, a sense of delight. I returned to my husband with my hands as bloodied as his. The noises and shouts of the night birds were all around.

Then, there was a knocking at the gate. It unnerved him but there was no need. We might have been seen in the nakedness of our love. We had to wash to free ourselves of the blood of the old King and get ready for the accession of the new. I had no worries, no concerns. This was our castle, my castle, which had been defiled by Duncan and we would make our accusations very clear. Those sons of Duncan would rue the day they came to my home. We would proclaim that Malcolm and Donalbain had killed their father since they could not wait for power. You see, we were inventing the truth. It's what those in power do. Duncan had lived in a world of lies. We were to live by our own truth. Scotland would thank us for the freedom we had restored. We would ensure peace through our politics, our diplomacy, and our moral righteousness.

After the body of the old King had been found, my husband became a little dramatic. He told everyone that in his rage he had slaughtered the guards who had neglected their duties in protecting King Duncan. I pretended to faint as he described the scene. It was perfect. My husband came to his senses. He would now bring stability even in the face of death and he would make Scotland a force in the world. We had triumphed. Scotland had triumphed. Scotland would be great again!"

Lady Macbeth sat back in her chair, satisfied that she had told me what she thought I needed to know. I listened to her tirade. She was luxuriating in the deed for which she was jointly responsible. I realised that tyranny could be a two-headed monster. She was as evil as her husband. There was a complexity to all of this, the complexity of understanding their relationship. In a sense, Duncan's bed was their bed, but his death was their rite of marriage and there was a post-coital sense of satisfaction within her. But I wondered, in destroying this man in his sleep, if ironically, they had destroyed their own relationship, which could have fostered life. Despite Duncan's evil, if that were true, had they abused the sanctity of life for which they would pay the psychological price at least? Did I feel pity for them? In a sense yes, since I realised that nothing could be the same for them. They had become defiled, as it were, by the murder of Duncan, whatever he had done to either of them. She had referred to 'my castle'. Did she mean her body? If so, what did that imply? Maybe she had said enough. I decided not to take it further. If they had destroyed their relationship as a couple, it was not my job to feel pity. It's my job, where possible, to allow my clients to find their own way through their difficulties. But how can you do that with those who have clearly committed murder, whatever the cause? How could anyone help a murderer? Maybe Duncan wasn't innocent but his was a life that had been butchered. Maybe he was, as they made out, manipulatively hypocritical but did that give them any kind of exoneration for the deed? There was no nobility in that murder and yet at the end of this narrative of theirs, as I knew, there was going to be a philosophical speech by Macbeth about the insignificance of life itself. Why would Macbeth then be allowed to die nobly, in single-armed combat, the benefit of which he had certainly not afforded Duncan? What I had suspected before I'd travelled to this place, was largely proving to be the case.

Evil was triumphing. But was this merely in fiction, in a play on the stage or was it more significant than that? Were the messages I was getting through my meetings with Macbeth and Lady Macbeth reflecting not only the realities of their time but indeed of my own? In all of this where did I lie and what danger was I in, a man of colour, in whom the King of England and Scotland had, let us say, taken an interest at Wilton?

JOURNAL

I was receiving information regularly from Amelia as to how towns and cities in several war zones were being attacked by drones and rockets, often through the night, whilst people were sleeping or saying goodnight to their children or perhaps making love to each other. Their lives were being snuffed out in an instant and yet unlike confident Duncan, they had been living, night after night, in the fear that this might happen.

Tyranny has many faces, some of which are not easily revealed. Macbeth and Lady Macbeth murdered sleep itself, their own relationship with each other, as well as the lives of those they had murdered. All that they did for each other 'signified nothing'. Whatever their excuses, they were part of a social structure which they fractured in their murder of sleep.

I recalled from another narrative that there was a man named Nomachi, an innocent working man in a country at war. Was it his war? No, it was a politician's war. He got on with his job day after day and went home every evening. On the morning of 6th August 1945 at 8.16, he became a burnt-out shadow on a pavement in the city named Hiroshima. If by destroying one city, with one irreversible act, it saved others from dying, was it morally justified? All war murders sleep by making it endless – like shadows burnt into a footpath.

I wasn't just giving psychotherapeutic help to Macbeth and Lady Macbeth, I was trying to learn what the dark side of humanity really looked like.

CHAPTER 37

L
ady Macbeth's exhilaration in telling me the story of
Duncan's murder didn't last long. As I answered the
door to her, on her next visit, Lady Macbeth pushed
past me and strode straight into my room. She was clearly
distressed. She stood in the middle of the room and begged me
to see her husband as soon as possible. She thought he was
going to do something terrible and that he needed my help. I
told her that I could only help clients if they came to me and
were prepared to talk. However, that was the point, Macbeth
was refusing to talk with her or with anyone else. She believed
that he had decided on a course of action, which she feared was
imminent. But when I asked her what kind of action, she
started to cry. "I don't know," she said, "but I fear it is not good.
He just won't discuss anything with me."

I made it clear that I was a psychotherapist, not a marriage
counsellor and that really, I should not have seen them both
together. I should have kept them strictly as individuals. She
was asking me to mediate between the two of them. I could not
do that. But since she was with me, I told her that I would listen
to her. She said that Macbeth had somehow gone into himself.
He wouldn't communicate with anyone and she was frightened

that he was about to commit a crime in order to consolidate his Kingship. I asked what action that might be and she said that he could be plotting to have Banquo killed. I noted that for her the killing of Banquo would be seen as a crime whilst the killing of Duncan had not been so. But surely what was going on was merely a continuation of the self-justification of murder for the crown of Scotland. Banquo was a threat. Why was this decision anything other than what could be expected? Of course, I couldn't say all this to her. I suspected that she'd never been totally open about her reason for wanting Duncan dead. I had to probe as to what the real issue was for her. In relation to Macbeth's change in behaviour, she repeated that it was because Macbeth wasn't involving her in any decisions.

"Has he told you that he's going to kill someone?"

"Not exactly," she replied.

"What do you mean?"

"I mean he has told me that he doesn't feel safe in his role as Monarch and needs to do something for his security. But he says that I don't need to know about it."

She was a troubled lady as she had started wringing her hands in anguish. She couldn't keep still. Walking around the room, touching items, rearranging my papers here and there, glaring at the mirror or the window or the door.

"Are you sleeping together?" I asked.

"No," she replied. "We did share adjoining chambers after the coronation but I am now in a different wing of the castle, known as the Queen's wing."

"And does he visit?"

"No," she replied.

"I saw him in the throne room and was about to ask why I was no longer welcome in his bed. But that's when he mentioned the need to consolidate his position. I can't handle this on my own."

"What do you suggest I can do for you?"

"I want you to be my doctor. You're a doctor, aren't you?"

"I'm a psychotherapist and a clinical Psychologist."

"But you are called 'Doctor'", she said. "You are our Doctor from today onwards. Come as our Doctor to a banquet, which I have arranged for the King. If you come, you can see what kind of state he is in."

"No," I said firmly. I am not your medical doctor. You have one already and you must use him. But as far as the banquet is concerned, I would be happy to come not as a guest but as an observer." Reluctantly she agreed and left my consulting room.

This had become a situation beyond my experience. Lady Macbeth was attempting to draw me into the play. I felt that I could not allow myself to become a character in the theatrical activities, in which my clients were employed. I felt so uneasy, that I decided to inform Amelia immediately about my dilemma.

Dear Amelia

My situation out here is difficult, to say the least. In my determination only to listen, there has been an unexpected attempt to involve me in the play as a character. It is because my two clients appear to be falling into a chasm. I need your advice to see me through this issue. I am already within the bounds of two realities and now I am being drawn into a third. I feel I am distancing myself from who I am.

Love Jacob

My dearest Jacob

You are there to find the facts as they occur, not as you interpret them through history or through fiction. You are seeing how things come to be and how things can be interpreted in different ways. You need to keep listening. This is the way you may discover the answers to the questions that prompted your journey. Keep listening. Keep discovering. There is always so much to learn. Just keep to your quest.

Love Amelia.

JOURNAL

You would not believe it if you read this in a story or saw it in the cinema. Why was I here if not to test the culture of the time against that of my own? Not only Macbeth's but the Scottish King's marriage wasn't in the best state. More details about his relationship with his Danish wife were emerging in London gossip. It was rumoured that one of the miscarriages which the Queen had, was self-induced because not only did the King refuse her access to her son, Prince Henry, but also, she argued over a royal protocol. She wanted to breastfeed her children. The Scottish King had determined that other traditional arrangements would be made to look after the Royal Issue. The Scottish King needed his Queen to follow due protocol. If royalty loses its protocols, it loses its identity as being 'set apart'.

The Scottish Queen from Denmark was a woman with her own desires which led to a standoff with her husband. There was unhappiness, self-harm, and the loss of a child in her womb. The Queen upheld the rights of women over their own bodies. There may have been many women at the time, who wanted that sort of Independence for themselves, but were not in an exalted enough position to demand that freedom. As some 21st century royals have found to their detriment, royal protocols overrule their individual desires, ambitions, freedoms and even at times their lives. They might flee to Paris or California, but can they ever really escape?

CHAPTER 38

With some reluctance, I did go as an observer to the banquet which Lady Macbeth had arranged. I refused, however, to be involved in any way. I would just watch the proceedings as if I were a spectator or advisor invited to a rehearsal of a play, which is exactly what I was.

At first, all seemed to go well. Macbeth welcomed his guests asking them to take their seats at the table. He seemed calm and at ease with being the host. But then he was summoned to talk to a rather disreputable-looking character. When he returned, he lamented the fact that Banquo hadn't arrived. He then said that he couldn't find a place to sit at the table and much to everyone's surprise, he went into a rage, asking who had done this. But what was 'this'? The guests stood up, waiting for their host to sit. Lady Macbeth tried to bring peace to the situation by saying that her husband had had these fits since childhood and that people should not be concerned and should sit down again. She spoke quietly to Macbeth as the guests were served, but I listened to what she was saying. He was clearly hallucinating again. This time about a ghost, who had taken his place, his chair, at the table. Lady Macbeth pacified her husband and he apologised to the guests. But then he went into a fit again. There was nothing to be done. The guests were dismissed. I decided to look for the 'disreputable looking character', who I had seen delivering a message to Macbeth.

I found him in the kitchens. After some careful questioning, he told me that Banquo was dead but his son Fleance had fled. He didn't admit that he had been involved in the killing, but I presumed that he had. Macbeth was obviously stressed because his plan had been frustrated. Although Banquo was dead, his son had escaped and could live to produce heirs, as foretold by the witches. The stress manifested itself in hallucinations with him seeing 'Banquo' sitting in Macbeth's chair, whichever one it was.

The next day Lady Macbeth came to see me.

"You saw what happened last night," she said. I replied that I had seen her husband at the banquet. She said that I had certainly failed through my 'mind talk', to heal her husband's troubled mind. He was to have no more of me but had rather gone off to take advice from the witches. They would put him right in the way that I could not. He was on a course of action over which neither of us had any control. She confirmed that Banquo was dead and more deaths would surely follow. Her eyes were filling with tears. "He doesn't listen to me or confide in me anymore," she said. With that, she wrung her hands together, stared at them and walked out without another word.

CHAPTER 39

T he news of the assault on Macduff's Castle and the slaughter of his wife and children was at first confused. Some said that Macduff, a known opponent of Macbeth, had been killed, while others said that he had been taken away and imprisoned. News travelled fast and rumours were rife so it was difficult to distinguish truth from rumour. Later I discovered the facts.

Macbeth had visited the witches again and one had warned him,

"*Beware Macduff.* This message was clear. However, the other prophesies were confusing. A second witch had said,

"*Be bloody bold and resolute, for none of woman born shall harm Macbeth."* Macbeth wondered how that could be since all humans are born of women. Then the third witch stated,

"*Macbeth shall never vanquished be, until Great Birnam Wood to High Dunsinane Hill shall come."*

Macbeth could not think how a wood could move. It could spread of course, but that would take years. He took comfort from these prophecies, which calmed his evil mind. Macduff was a threat to Macbeth and like most tyrants in history he decided that Macduff and his family and anyone remaining in his way would be eliminated. So, he gave orders to, kill, kill and kill.

When the murderers arrived, Macduff wasn't in the castle. He had left his wife and children to go and find Malcolm, to persuade him to fight Macbeth for the throne, as promised by Duncan. The assassins murdered Lady Macduff and her children, who were there.

As it happened, when the news of this came through, I'd just received a message from Amelia.

Dear Jacob,

Some awful things are happening in the world that you left. First, there was the invasion in Eastern Europe, a deliberate land grab. It was supposed to be a short, sharp 'operation' but the invaded people fought back. In retaliation rockets and drones continually bombard innocent civilians. Women and children are being murdered in their homes while the men are away at the frontline fighting as soldiers. The killings are senseless. Tyranny and pride have taken over from care and duty, just as in other wars through the ages.

Who is to blame? I point my finger firmly at the tyrants, but also at the politicians who have failed to comprehend how war can be avoided. Century after century ordinary people have been sacrificed on the orders of the ruling classes and still it goes on. Now another war has escalated in Gaza. Rebels attacked Israel and Israel has retaliated. Civilian casualties are enormous. Thousands of innocent lives are being lost. There seems no end to these atrocities, which have taken over from other wars in the news. I wish you were here since I feel quite distracted and desolate about the failure of mankind to find peace and to keep peace.

All my love Amelia

JOURNAL

I wondered what difference there was between the tyranny that I was witnessing with Macbeth, with the Scottish King of England and with those in Amelia's world. The Scottish King was having Catholics and homosexuals rounded up and killed. Women who attempted to display their individuality were being condemned as witches and mercilessly hanged. Men sent by the Government were raiding the homes of suspected Catholics and arresting them, some of whom would then end up dead. The Scottish King, who had assumed the Crown in England, had displayed the pride of a family, which eventually would lead to insurrection – a civil war in which fathers might kill their sons or sons kill their fathers. I wanted to cry out at the top of my voice from one age to another from one century to another, 'Stop you barbarians. Stop you evil men and put your heads into your hands with shame. Stop I say'. But as I know, the Civil War would come, a King would lose his head and a Puritanical tyrant would rule the country. He would close the theatres and abolish Christmas. After his death, a new Monarch would take over and have the tyrant's decaying corpse hung up over the entrance to Parliament. How sick can we get as human beings?

Am I simply failing to understand human nature? What is it with tyrants? What is it they want? Is it just an inevitable desire for power, followed by a period of totally cold thought? We have studied tyranny in so many leaders from Tamburlaine to Hitler, Mussolini, Franco and Stalin and an array of them in the 21st century. We can study their behaviour. Indeed, we have to study it to be able to warn about its development. But even with this knowledge, it seems that we cannot stop the accession or behaviour of tyrants. Indeed, sometimes we even vote for them! It is only after their election that we discover how they will abuse their power. We realise our mistake when it is too late.

But for now, I need to wake up and concentrate on the world of the seventeenth century which I am inhabiting. Why did I come here if not to find out more about Macbeth and in doing so, more about myself? Isn't that what Amelia has been telling me?

CHAPTER 40

T here was a knocking at the door. It was a cold day. I thought that it would be Will but I was surprised to see Macduff. I greeted him warmly. I expected him to talk about his grief over his wife and family or his need for revenge, but you never can tell what people want to discuss. He sat down and as usual, I waited for the client to begin. He took me by surprise,

"I want to ask you a hypothetical question," he said.

"No problem," I answered.

"How can you tell a lie from a truth?"

"That's a philosophical question, not a hypothetical one," I answered.

"No matter," he responded continuing, "Say that a man who wanted to be King of Scotland had confided in you that he was unworthy to be King."

I was puzzled and frowned as I couldn't understand what he was trying to say but I remained silent. He picked up on my facial expression. He looked around the room and at the window to make sure no one was listening. "Let's say that this person stated that he had none of the kingly qualities, such as Justice, Verity, Temperance, Stableness, Bounty, Perseverance,

Mercy, Lowliness, Devotion, Patience, Courage, Fortitude and that he was an avaricious fake, who was deceitful, malicious and most of all lustful and uncaring for anyone but himself. What would you say?" I didn't reply, so he continued, "Why would he say such awful things about himself if he wanted to be King?" Again, I didn't reply but thought to myself, that the description wasn't far off some rulers whom I'd come across in history, but that was irrelevant. What mattered was what Macduff was saying and what was going through his mind. I still refrained from getting into a conversation with him.

Macduff, sitting in the chair opposite me, rubbed his face in anguish. "Say that this man," was so adamant that he made you believe that what he was saying was true, that he was luxuriating in the opposites of virtue. It was like someone who has committed a string of crimes might want his notoriety to bring him attention, baiting you to debate as to whether personal moral conduct was important in a leader. Is it? Doesn't political leadership require strong men, not necessarily good ones? What would you say? Dr Fortune, what would you say?" He shrugged, disappointed that he couldn't draw me in.

"What would you say?" he asked again.

I thought to myself that he would be a person unfit for kingship. But was this true? Could one overlook a leader's faults or even his crimes? I would find that hard to do. However, I turned the question back to Macduff and asked,

"Could you tolerate an evil man as a leader?"

Macduff fell into silence. This was a man in grief about his nation and his family. He'd lost his wife and his children through the actions of a tyrant. What comfort can be given to those in such mourning? There was none. Was he displaying emotional turmoil in a political arena to relieve his personal pain? Was he trying to assuage himself? Angry, with his face in his hands, he was breathing heavily. He looked up at me and cried,

"O Scotland, Scotland….. Fit to govern? No, not to live…

when shalt thou see thy wholesome days again?" He told me that these were the words he said to Malcolm, the son of the dead King Duncan, who had been murdered by Macbeth. All their rulers were as bad as each other.

But then Macduff told me incredulously, that Malcolm suddenly denied what he had said and told him that he, Malcolm, was the exact opposite in his life and demeanour. He had made up this story to find out where Macduff's loyalty lay. Malcolm went on to explain his behaviour by saying that Macbeth had been sending people to try and trick him. That was why he felt he needed to test Macduff's integrity. It was such a strange thing to do as Malcolm now started a litany of his virtues, which were in direct contradiction to what he had just said!

"Where is the truth, Doctor Fortune and where are the lies? Then, whilst I was in such confusion, the Thane of Ross appeared and told me that my family were 'well at rest' when he had left them."

At this point, the poor man in front of me broke out into tears, which had been welling up for some time.

"At rest when he had left them," Macduff repeated. "Why play around with the truth? This was equivocation, a linguistic trick. In the end, he confessed that my castle had been surprised, my wife and all my children, my innocent, pretty children, had been slaughtered by the tyrant Macbeth." He paused, pulling himself together before saying, "That was the fact, not words covering up, deceiving with false conclusions. Facts and truths – when people are dead, they are dead. That is a fact." He looked at me hard, before stating coldly, "I'll kill that bastard, even if it is the last thing that I do."

I presumed that Macduff was referring to Macbeth, although Malcolm had shown the deviousness of an accomplished politician, playing with truth to such an extent that you couldn't distinguish it from a lie, or even a bluff from a double bluff. Language was being undermined and fiction had merged with reality.

I was in the company of a broken man. Nothing could console him except for the primitive desire of an eye for an eye. He stood up and walked to the window, looking out and then back at me saying coldly, "I do not know if Malcolm is a good man or a bad man. But I do know that Macbeth murdered my wife and children and I'll be revenged." I stared at him eye to eye across the room, but then looked away because I realised that he needed to say more. I poured some sack for him to drink and he sat down again. I needed to wait for him to reveal out loud what he was thinking.

"What kind of man am I?" he asked, "Am I a traitor?"

He pulled at a fastening on his sleeve, which had come loose. Eventually, it came off and fell on the floor. Spikey shot out from under the cupboard and looked round the room, wanting to see what had made the noise. Macduff picked up the fastening and passed it from one hand to the other. Spikey turned away and went back under the cupboard.

"People talk about traitors," he began again, "As if they know what they are but do they?" He looked up at me. "A traitor is one who breaks his vow. I broke my vow and I was a traitor to my marriage, to my responsibility to my wife and my children. I left them alone in the castle. I came in search of help to rid Scotland of its tyrant King. This King to whom all the Thanes had sworn allegiance at Scone. I had gone to Fife, not Scone and I hadn't sworn any form of allegiance. I wouldn't swear loyalty to that man Macbeth. But in *his* mind, I had shown disloyalty. I should have been true to him as King but I was absent from his coronation." He paused again, looking towards the door. "He is now King of Scotland just as Duncan was King of Scotland when Macdonald, Cawdor and the other Thanes rebelled and joined the Norwegian invaders. Now I am with Malcolm, who has allied with an English army, prepared for a new invasion against a lawful, if tyrannical,

King. What is the truth in all of that? Am I doing what Macdonald had done? I am allying with a foreign force against the legitimacy of Macbeth's kingship, irrespective of his evil. I was a traitor to my wife and to the legally anointed King, who no doubt would claim that he was divinely called to Majesty by God.

Who was Malcolm? Had he been acclaimed King at Scone? Of course, he hadn't. Malcolm had merely been promised by Duncan that he could be the next King. He confused me by confessing that he had told me lies to trick me. How can you be sure of the truth with someone who does that?"

Macduff was in total anguish and I knew he would just go round and round with this argument in his head. What use would that be to him? I had to speak.

"Don't give up," I said, "On being true to yourself because you can't be true until you know yourself."

"And how do I do that?"

"That is a matter for you not me. I'm not here to tell you what to do. I have said enough, if not too much. I'm not a preacher but a psychotherapist. I can't heal peoples' souls if they exist."

Slowly and sadly Macduff got up and left. I watched him going down the road towards the river and the bridge where the traitors' heads are left on spikes to warn all not to rebel against the legitimate King. I wondered what makes a King legitimate. As Will ironically comments elsewhere, "a fine word 'legitimate'?"

JOURNAL

One wrong decision can cause a myriad of problems, affecting people who do not know the decision, will never know it, or do not want to know it. Macbeth decided to murder Duncan and one ramification was that later Lady Macduff and her children were slaughtered. So why should Macbeth be afforded a tragic, heroic end? This was an issue that had bugged me from the start of my adventure. I was still puzzled by it.

Then, thinking about the Jacobean court, what might have happened if Robert Cecil had not decided to have the Scottish King crowned King of England? The long-term consequences of that decision for the nation, and for that matter for the Scottish King's family, would have been very different. His son Henry, may not have died of typhoid in London in 1612, aged only 18 and full of promise. He was influenced by his mother, who was devoted to the Arts. In the year of which I'm now recording, 1606, he was just 12 years old.

But what is the point of thinking 'what if?' Decisions are made by those with power and we the underlings benefit or suffer the consequences. Henry VIII's break with Rome led to many unnecessary executions and hardships, mainly for those wanting the return of the Old Faith but also at times for supporters of the new Church, especially when Mary Tudor took the throne.

In my day in the 21st century, the United Kingdom's break from Europe, engineered by slogans and some blatant lies and exaggerations, threatened the livelihoods of many whilst the political elite grew rich and appeared to receive significant benefits. Politicians who genuinely think of the people first are rare whatever the form of government. Undermine the language and you undermine the stability of the country.

CHAPTER 41

K nock, knock, knock.

"Who's there in the psychotherapist's name?" I expected someone from the rehearsals, Malcolm perhaps or Macduff and was, therefore, surprised to see Augustine. I shook his hand, showed him in and offered him a cup of tea, which he accepted as he made himself comfortable. He told me that the date, 7th August 1606 had now been confirmed for the Royal performance of *Macbeth* at Hampton Court Palace. It was to be staged before the King of Scotland and the King of Denmark. It was doubtful that the Queen would attend, as she had other engagements.

The gossip was that the King had sighed when he heard that the play would be a tragedy by Shakespeare and the Queen had asked why it couldn't be a play by Ben Jonson, who was joyous and made her laugh. Augustine told me about the persistent rumour among the actors, that Thomas Middleton was to rewrite the Macbeth play. There had been some tense discussions among the actors.

"Shakespeare," John Heminges had said, "Wrote some of the best plays of Queen Elizabeth's reign and would do it for the new King."

"The King fell asleep in *Measure for Measure*," retorted John Grimble, who had been the understudy for the actor Burbage, in the play.

"Well, he won't fall asleep in this one." Armin insisted. "It's about Scotland and the King's heritage. It will exalt the new Monarch in the eyes of the Danish King and will re-establish Shakespeare as a great playwright."

"Was it because the King was going to attend the play that you brought in Middleton to help?" Grimble, mischievously, had asked Augustine, who immediately denied that it was he who had brought in Middleton. Augustine protested that the young dramatist, on his own volition, had written a speech for Hecate, the goddess of the witches, and some lines for the other witches and a song or two, but that was that! If he wanted to use those again, including songs in a later play of his own, he was at liberty to do so.

Augustine also told me that he made a pointed remark to Grimble, that in any case, they hadn't got a good enough actor to play an extended role of Hecate. I looked puzzled. Augustine laughed and continued, "Grimble wanted the role, but he's useless. If Grimble had been playing Angelo in *Measure for Measure* the King would have walked out, rather than fallen asleep. Anyway, we don't have to worry about his acting anymore as he's left the company and taken up a position with the Government."

At that, Augustine stopped talking and looked at me with concern, as a thought suddenly struck him. "Perhaps Grimble was always with the Government, maybe he was one of Cecil's men!"

"Highly likely," I said. "But why would Cecil allow him to leave the company if he had put him there?"

"Who knows?" Augustine replied. "Anyway, I understand that Will intends to call in to see you. Boost him up, will you?"

"How are the rehearsals going?"

"Very well. The actors are totally into their roles."

He thanked me for my help and the tea and went on his way.

Augustine's visit, however, had disturbed me. There was obviously unrest within the theatre as to the nature of their plays. The arrival of the Scots in London and more particularly the various demands of the Scottish King and Queen on the theatre companies meant that things were different from how they were in the time of Queen Elizabeth. Those now in power wanted more spectacle, more music, dancing and lavish masques as they had enjoyed in Scotland. Even the Scottish King had played in some of these.

In addition to this, there was the colour question. Maybe Shakespeare had tried to soften it and make it a less hostile image in *Othello*. There he created sympathy for the tragic figure of a black general duped by his white officer. But the idea behind *The Masque of Blackness* was uncertain, to say the least. Not that this had caused the postponement of the sequel, *The Mask of Beauty*. The financing of it was the problem as it often was with the Scottish King and his wife.

As far as the rumours concerning the King's sexual preferences were concerned, I had experienced his interest in me at Wilton. He certainly had taken, let us say, 'an interest in me' not just as a man, but as a 'black man'. What would I do if the Palace ever sent for me? That I was back in London was certainly known by the authorities and maybe even by the King. I had received a visit from the 'man from the Government' and I'm sure my consulting room had been searched. If summoned either I would have to go to the Palace or abandon my mission. But if I went, how would I handle the situation? There were rumours of the King's advances having been exercised in a variety of ways. Augustine had suggested that I needed to be careful. Amelia, no doubt, would tell me to return home but I resolved to continue to play my role and live with the consequences whatever they were.

I looked in the mirror. I certainly was of colour but I didn't think I looked that attractive. "Maybe mirrors lie," I said to myself, "Or maybe reflections don't matter."

CHAPTER 42

S ex is a driver, but for Macbeth and Lady Macbeth, sex was no longer a factor. Indeed, they hardly ever met but lived alone with their guilty secrets. Macbeth hung on to the riddles of the witches and he felt unassailable. Not even his guilt over the deaths of Duncan, Banquo or Macduff's wife and children could compete with his conviction of unassailability. His 'bible' was the witches' words and he believed that everything he had done had been necessary.

Lady Macbeth did not return to the consulting room. Her doctor came there to tell me that the Queen's ladies were now concerned for her health. She was sleepwalking and saying things that should remain hidden, even from thought. He reported that he had witnessed an episode of her walking and wringing her hands as if trying to wash stains from them. She was a lonely lady with no comfort and no friends. I wondered if the Scottish King would see in her a vision of his mother, whom he'd never met, even though he had given the outward appearance of mourning after her execution. What was the truth in all of that episode back in 1587? Was it Queen Elizabeth's Minister, Walsingham, who had deceived her into agreeing to the execution? Was it Robert Cecil's father? Did Elizabeth deny her own guilt over the death of an anointed Monarch? After her death, did she have a speech ready to exonerate herself before the pearly gates?

What an age of hypocrisy and cruelty was reflected in this play called *Macbeth*. There was an emblem of it all: Lady Macbeth, Queen of Scotland, wringing her hands, haunted by 'thick coming fancies', as Shakespeare called them, that kept her from her rest.

The doctor told me that Macbeth had wanted him to cure her, saying,

> Canst thou not minister to a mind diseased,
> Pluck from the memory a rooted sorrow,
> Raze out the written troubles of the brain,
> And with some sweet oblivious antidote
> Cleanse the stuffed bosom of that perilous stuff
> Which weighs upon the heart?

But the doctor, with all his training, could not do that, suggesting that only the patient can do it for themselves. He said that he felt helpless as he walked away sadly from my consulting rooms.

Later, I heard that Seyton, an evil-looking retainer, had reported to Macbeth that the Queen was dead. It was then that Macbeth uttered the famous lines,

> She should have died hereafter:
> There would have been time for such a word.
> Tomorrow, and tomorrow, and tomorrow,
> Creeps in this petty pace from day to day,
> To the last syllable of recorded time:
> And all our yesterdays have lighted fools
> The way to dusty death. Out, out, brief candle.
> Life's but a walking shadow, a poor player

That struts and frets his hour upon the stage
And then is heard no more. It is a tale
Told by an idiot, full of sound and fury
Signifying nothing.

Following the news of the Queen's death, Macbeth came to my consulting room and repeated the speech to me. I asked him if he believed that life signified nothing. He responded that this was a reaction to the death of his wife. But for him, maybe it would prove to be a passing emotion. The witches had given him three prophecies which he would hold on to until the end. Macbeth went on to say, "That is the man that I am. I fight to the end and that is my glory. That is what I signify. I am more than nothing. I am something. That will be proved because one day someone will write about me and actors will play me and once one performance is done another will take its place, and then others until the last syllable of recorded time. This motivates me to go on and fight to the death."

With that Macbeth said that my work was over. He left my room confidently striding back to the theatre.

A few moments later, there was another knocking at the door. It was Will, who appeared to be a bit flustered. The performance was the next day. He'd come because I'd asked to see him. I was still concerned that he may have gone too far in what he was doing. "Will," I said, "Are you sure you know what you are doing with this play and the politics surrounding it?"

"Yes, yes, my friend. You don't need to worry. As you know, this play of mine isn't all that it seems. It appears to flatter the King, but it does far more than that. I'm making fun of him by playing to his belief in witches and the way they behave. The witches all survive and the prophecies are proved to be true. The Scottish King sits there, thinking he is right to pursue such fiends and he'll be enjoying his self-righteousness. He will probably miss the fact that the witches triumph in defying Macbeth, the King of Scotland. They were not executed."

"I don't see any problem with that," I said, "but I noticed that you have called one of the nobles, Lennox, the first Duke of which was Esmé Stuart, one of the closest intimates of the Scottish King."

Will roared with laughter saying, "Yes! He was someone who gave cause for the Kirk to have the Scottish King kidnapped and imprisoned at Ruthven Castle, long before the later drama with the Gowrie brothers at the same place. But watching the play, the Scottish King won't realise that, since the character won't be named during the performance and he is a figure who at various times, argues both for and against Macbeth. Don't worry, I've taken care. No one else watching the play will detect what I have done. You, Jacob, are just too eagle-eyed, in looking out to help me"

"But why are you doing it Will?" I probed. "Is it just that you don't like the Scottish King or is it something else, like being a recusant Catholic, or seeming like one? Will, I am still worried that you may be playing with fire."

"Not at all, it is so well disguised that no one will detect what I've done. I'm an Elizabethan, loyal to the Queen I served, a Queen who laughed with us in our plays not at us for writing plays. But this fickle King has no feeling for us. He is interested not in the people but in himself. There is one rule for him and another for the rest of us. He exploits and discards those such as the Gowrie's. He sleeps with whom he pleases, whether they want him or not. He lives for power and authority and he makes a spectacle of death for the likes of Nicholas Owen and Henry Garnet and anyone else who speaks against him. So, let's just laugh at him, at the 'horrible sight' in the mirror. There is no more to it than that my friend. He'll never know. He is just too proud." With that, chuckling still, he took his leave saying as he left the room. "Note the name of Macbeth's servant."

"I didn't have to think about it. Take care," I said, "That Seyton doesn't come knocking at your door tomorrow."

"I will," Will replied, still laughing. I sat back and worried about what would happen the next day. There was going to be just one performance of the play at Hampton Court Palace. There is no record, as far as I know, of how the two Kings received it, except the one here in my recollections.

CHAPTER 43

The day of the event at Hampton Court Palace had arrived. The play was to be performed not in the Great Hall but in the gardens. Thankfully the weather was good and the sun was shining brightly. A slightly raised stage had been erected at the rear of the lawn. It had no backdrop except the wonderful flowers in the garden. Throughout the performance, the actors were to wait for their entrances at the sides of the stage, in full view of the audience. I'd been invited by Augustine to join them and the stagehands, which meant that I'd see the play side on. The guests who made up the audience were seated in two blocks on the right and left with a passage between them. The people closest to the front, such as the Earl of Pembroke, had been provided with chairs. Behind them, benches had been set out. At the rear, there was room for Palace employees to stand. Right at the front, immediately facing the stage, were two thrones, one decorated with the crest of Denmark and the other with the crests of England and Scotland. Before the performance, the two Kings enjoyed a private dinner in the Palace, with rich food and good wine.

When they entered the garden from the Palace ready for the

performance, the audience stood as the Kings proceeded down the aisle. They greeted those on the left and the right with nods and royal waves. At one point, Denmark stumbled but didn't quite fall thanks to an attentive guard. The Scottish King not noticing, continued down the aisle slightly in front of his brother-in law. But reaching the thrones, he sat on the wrong one. The officials couldn't believe it and they quickly informed the King of his error.

"I've taken your throne, Denmark," he laughed, as Denmark arrived at the other one, puzzling about the twin crests.

"Is that why I've got England and Scotland?" he asked. The Kings were then shown to their correct thrones by the officials, who served them more wine.

The play began with the weird sisters saying,

When shall we three meet again?
In thunder, lightning, or in rain?

When the hurly-burly's done
When the battle's lost, and won.

At this, I overheard the Scottish King say to the Danish one, "I detest witches. In Scotland, we burn them alive but in soft old England they are merely hanged." To this, Denmark replied,

"I don't think we have witches in my country, but I really don't know."

"I'm sure you'll see what we do with them here in England. They'll be hanged at the end of the play, mark my words." With that, they settled back into their thrones and showed some interest in the drama. Every now and again I heard them commenting to each other about it.

"It's the woman's fault. She is headstrong!" said the Scottish King.

"Just like my sister," commented Denmark.

"Shush, she might be here incognito. You never can tell with her," laughed the Scottish King. After a while he said, "A few traitors here in London tried to assassinate me but as you can see, they didn't get away with it. They tried to blow me up, but I caught them and they were hanged and butchered like animals. They were Catholics, of course."

"Yes, you've told me."

After a little more of the play, the Scottish King became restless, saying, "I don't think it's right to kill the King of Scotland in this play. What do you think Denmark? He seems like a good man to me. I wonder if the Master of the Revels has seen this?"

"I don't like that either, but I suppose it's history. I'm sure it will be put right in the end." Denmark replied.

"Maybe, but I'm not happy about it." Scotland started to make a move as if he might leave, but Denmark restrained him and signalled for more wine.

"Sit back. It's only a play and this Porter at the gate is funny. He is talking about the death of an equivocator."

"Oh, that'll be the Jesuit, Garnet," came the reply. "We hanged him. I watched him die in secret of course, but I had a good view. The old traitor struggled but he died in the end, with hangers-on pulling at his legs."

The play progressed to the scene in which Macbeth goes to the witches to seek information about the future. This was where the company had planned to 'honour' the new Scottish King by the procession of eight Kings of Scotland, at the end of which the mirror would be shown to the Scottish King, reflecting him in his lineage to his guests and the audience behind.

In preparation for the performance there had been a question about the props. What kind of mirror should they use to allow the King not merely to see himself but to show the reflection to the whole of the audience? In the Palace, there was one room which had a pair of mirrored doors, just one of which would be perfect for the play. The Palace Chamberlain, after some convincing, allowed the actors to take it. They had explained that they wanted to give the King a surprise. But once they had taken the door, they found that it was too heavy for the eighth apparition to hold up. It was therefore decided that the three witches would bring on the mirror from off-stage.

The scene started just as planned with the heirs of Banquo leading the stately procession. My anxieties about this scene remained with me as I watched. From the rear, the first king entered, then the second, a third, a fourth, all walking in a stately manner down the centre of the stage, looking straight ahead before turning off to the right in front of the thrones; a fifth came, a sixth and a seventh. Now would come the eighth, followed by the three witches carrying the mirrored door, which would show the King's reflection, allowing him to bask in his glory. Macbeth in character would turn away, crying out "Horrible Sight." So entranced and anxious was I that I hadn't noticed that both the Scottish King and the King of Denmark had fallen asleep during the boring prelude to the scene, in which Hecate had given a long speech, followed by an extended dialogue between Lennox and an unnamed Lord.

The two Kings were in dreamland, curled up on their thrones in foetal positions. The witches came downstage, carrying the mirrored door with its back to the audience. They turned it to the right and then to the left until they reached the foot of the stage. I realised that they were about to turn it so the mirror faced the Scottish King, which would have shown him in his drunken comatose state. What could be done? This would make him and his brother-in-law a laughing stock. Had Macbeth noticed? He was well into his role. The moment came and I looked around for help. A voice rang out from close to me,

"Macbeth, Macbeth, hit the back of the mirror!" Macbeth looked up and immediately on seeing what was happening, with a swipe of his sword he hit the back of the mirror as hard as he could, letting out an almighty expletive as he did so.

The three witches dropped the mirror and its glass shattered onto the floor in front of the Kings. They turned a third time and fled the stage. Macbeth instinctively bent down to pick up the jigsaw of pieces of the mirror from the floor, which were reflecting numerous images of himself. The noise had woken up the Kings, who saw Macbeth in front of them, seemingly bowing. So they, thinking it was the end of the play, started to applaud. The audience, taking their cue from the Kings, also clapped. The actors realising what had happened, came onto the stage joining Macbeth in taking a bow. The Scottish King looked at the King of Denmark and signalled that they should leave. Acknowledging the cast with royal, if alcoholic waves, they exited through the grounds back into the Palace. The rest of their guests followed.

The Scottish King was overheard saying drunkenly,

"Wha' you shink of that Denmark?"

"Pershaps more mushic 'n dancin', 'n' shum acra… acro… acrobatics from the wishes!"

"That Shshshakespeare – no imashination!"

Meanwhile, the actors all gathered around Richard Burbage who had been playing Macbeth. He had cut himself slightly as he tried to pick up some of the glass.

"That was a good call," said Burbage, as one of the actors came to bandage his hand. "It would have been the end of us if we had reflected the King in that state to the audience." He started to laugh. "What a horrible sight!"

"It was lucky," said Augustine, "That the witches only did two turns. Otherwise, the mirror would have been facing the Kings."

It was then that I realised what had happened. "Two turns," I said, "But in order to flee the stage they did another turn!" Everyone looked at me perplexed.

"What do you mean?" Burbage asked.

"Well," I said, "You hit the back of the stage mirror which had formerly been a door and you swore. Don't you understand? There were three turns, an expletive and a knock at the stage's door. It is the start of a theatrical superstition about this 'bloody play'. I was so excited that I joyfully put my hands in the air and started to dance.

"Have you gone mad Jacob?" Augustine asked. "We don't know what you're talking about. It's bad luck because we'll have to pay for the mirror, which will cost us a fortune."

"No," a voice said, "I'll pay for it." Pembroke, who'd returned from the Palace to congratulate them all continued, "I heard and saw what happened. I wondered if the Kings were asleep as I could hear them breathing heavily. It would have been a disaster if they had been exposed. Who called to Burbage to hit the back of that mirrored door?"

"It was me, Sir," answered Alfred.

"Oh, Lady Macbeth! Well done." Pembroke smiled and asked, "Aren't you Augustine's boy, who nearly died in a fire?"

"That was at my parent's house, Sir. But now I live with Mr and Mrs Phillips."

"I know. You were alert and very good in what you did, but you were even better in your portrayal of Lady Macbeth."

Alfred beamed as did his stepfather Augustine, who gave him a hug. All the actors and stagehands were around us as this conversation occurred. I realised that maybe this was the origin of the rumour, that the boy playing Lady Macbeth had died before the first performance. Stories get retold and refashioned as time goes on and Pembroke's question about a 'boy that nearly died,' may well have, through time, become 'the boy that died before the play', as Max Beerbohm had reiterated in the 19th century.

However, I was in no doubt that the origin of the superstitious ritual came about because of that day's performance in which bad luck had turned into good.

As Pembroke left to go into the Palace, he whispered to Augustine,

"I overheard the two Kings say that they would have preferred more music and acrobatics from the witches, who then should have died at the end. But overall, they were delighted."

"Thank you. We'll think about that!"

We noticed that the sky was clouding over and it was starting to rain. In the distance we could hear thunder.

"It's a good job the play ended early," Burbage said. "I don't know about the rest of you, but I am thirsty." As the thunder moved closer, we all made for the nearest tavern and drank almost as much wine as the two Kings had imbibed that day, although perhaps that was impossible!

JOURNAL

The next day I sent a report to Amelia, telling her what had happened. She sent a letter back to me.

Dearest Jacob

Thank you for your report on the first performance of *Macbeth*. Despite the mishaps, it seems that all went well and at least the two Kings left happily enough. It is strange how superstitions start and you were right to go back to the beginning.

I've been doing some research of my own while you are away. Shakespeare's godson, William Davenant, revived *Macbeth* in 1664, at the new Duke's Theatre, four years after the restoration of the Monarchy. He added music and more witches with them singing, dancing and even flying. Today I understand, that would have also happened if Sir Ralph's production had gone ahead. Unfortunately, it has been permanently withdrawn owing to the length of the actor's convalescence.

I have also discovered that the great actor David Garrick in the 18th century thought, as you do, that the tragic heroic death of Macbeth was inappropriate. So, he tried to restore the play to something like its original. He decided, however, that such an evil man should die in the manner of Marlowe's Doctor Faustus, a soul unable to repent and only fit for the horrors of hell. He wrote a soliloquy, modelled on Marlowe's, with the final words,

I dare not ask for mercy

It is too late, hell drags me down. I sink,

I sink – oh – my soul is lost forever!

Oh! (dies.)

Good for Garrick perhaps, except that Marlowe was a much better poet!

I'm looking forward to your return home whenever that may be. You have been away too long.

All my love,

Amelia.

Dear Amelia

Perhaps Will deliberately avoided a Faustian ending, preferring not to have his play compared with Marlowe's, but I think it may be more than dramatic comparison. Perhaps I'll never know unless I find an opportunity to ask Will outright.

I am almost satisfied that my quest is nearing its end. Spikey and I hope to be with you soon.

My love

Jacob.

CHAPTER 44

S ome days after we had returned from Hampton Court by riverboat, Will and I were talking in my consulting room. He had mixed feelings about what had occurred at the Palace. He was relieved by the mirror episode, which had brought an unexpected ending to the performance. If it weren't for that, the Scottish King would have been humiliated and Will would have been blamed. Heaven knows what would have happened to him, perhaps he would have been caught up in a fight over the bill in a tavern and killed as a result, or maybe he would have had an accident at the Globe, falling from a window on the upper gallery onto the stage. Or, possibly he would have just been taken into the Tower and racked to teach him a lesson. As history shows, you don't mess with tyrants and you certainly don't humiliate them.

So, he was grateful for what had happened but then again there was nearly half the play still to go, when the two Kings had left the garden, bringing the performance to an abrupt end.

"I had written some lines," he said to me, "which were not uttered at Hampton Court, but which sum up the state of our land, or any land, under the rule of the self-obsessed leader, whether a king or tyrant:

Each new mourn
New widows howl, new orphans cry, new
   sorrows
Strike Heaven on the face.

"Exactly," I replied. "It shows the self-centred character of a tyrant since in the end the tyrant thinks only of himself. Macbeth even ignored Lady Macbeth, who sleepwalked and was haunted by the horror of the murders that had occurred." I explained that I had worked with Lady Macbeth in preparation for the sleepwalking scene, trying to ensure that her mind was in turmoil and could find no peace by facing up to what had been done.

But, I continued, "Macbeth on the other hand, makes his statement about the life signifying nothing yet you give him a warrior's death to be killed in battle. Why give him a heroic type of death? Why not give him a Faustian death on stage?"

Will shrugged, "I see your problem. Faust is a scholar but Macbeth is a warrior and a tyrant, fighting is in his blood. It is almost as if death, other people's deaths, are his business. He dies because of how he has lived. It is as simple as that. You live by the sword and you die by the sword. In tragedy, the death of the main character is the usual ending, whether that character is a tyrant or a martyr to a cause. Some might argue that they can be both. Does he believe that life is insignificant? Perhaps he does, since he has killed so many and now is killed by another warrior with hate in his heart. For the tyrant, Macbeth, his life has signified something and nothing. He wanted to become a King and succeeded. But once he was King, it didn't turn out as he wanted, proving it to be nothing. He was a hero in battle but was a tyrant as a Monarch. It might be argued that this is what heroism and tyranny have in common. There are two opposite aspects of one person, which coincide in the manner of his death, bringing his evil to an end, off-stage."

"But Will," I asked, "do you think evil can come to an

end?" He thought for a while and said, "I don't know. I seem to be in a labyrinth of darkness from which I cannot escape even though I allow an escape in death for my protagonists – whether they be Othello, King Lear, or indeed Macbeth.

I wondered, as he sat there in my room, how society was changing under the Scottish King. I raised the question with him.

He answered "Life isn't the same, but I tell you, Jacob, that it will come to a bad end for this Scottish King and his family. If you do not show mercy, mercy will not be shown to you. Maybe it will not be him that suffers but sooner or later some will revolt against this Stuart family for good or for bad." I merely nodded. Then as he went to leave the room, I asked,

"What next?" He reached the door and turned, answering,

"Lovers, Jacob. Mature lovers who revolt against the Empire, which they had hoped they could control."

"Sounds good to me," I replied and with that, he left, not to go to the theatre but to return to his home in Stratford, for a while at least. There he could research the story of *Antony and Cleopatra* in the quiet solitude of his own library.

PART III
THE PSYCHOTHERAPIST

CHAPTER 45

Amelia had informed me that Ever and Jackie were on the way back to the consulting room, to return to London in the 21st century. I was looking forward to seeing them.

There was a knocking at my door. I wondered if it might be them but why would they knock? I opened the door and recognised a Scotsman. He was not the one of my apparitions, that figure had vanished some time ago after I'd left Wiltshire, when my mind was more at ease. This man I recognised as the young Scottish riding companion of the King.

"You may remember me," he said, "From your cottage at Wilton House. My name is Robert Kerr."

"I do," I said, "please come in. "You were the young man who brought His Majesty into the cottage and looked after him."

He smiled and said, "I seem to remember that you were the one who helped His Majesty. He wishes to see you immediately. Come with me now."

"I'd be delighted," I said, lying. My heart sank as I remembered those visits which the King made to my cottage, coming secretly to see me. I wondered if Kerr was there on those other unrecorded occasions, watching from the woods. I'd certainly recognised his name from history. He was to become one of the King's closest advisers possibly even a lover, but the relationship had not quite reached that level of privilege yet.

As we left the consulting room and walked towards the river, I asked Kerr if he could tell me why the King wanted to see me. He said that he didn't know and I believed him. We crossed the bridge. It seemed that the blackened heads of the traitors were looking down on me. Black, I remembered, was the 'devil's colour', but the heads may have been those of saintly men, caught up in the accusations following the gunpowder plot. I couldn't tell. They were all dead now.

At the end of the bridge, we kept straight on, past the turnings for the Blackfriars Theatre and St Paul's Cathedral. We turned left towards St Mary's Le Bow. We passed the Royal Exchange and then on through the markets of Cheapside. Some people, seeing my colour, as usual deliberately bumped into me, to touch my skin and indeed some children watching dared each other to do so. This was nothing new to me, but Kerr commented upon it with some unease. He didn't want to bring me to the King dishevelled and maybe even bruised. I shuddered as I saw Ludgate prison and yet another execution yard, with Newgate in the distance. We continued into Fleet Street and down the Strand towards Whitehall Palace. Then we veered to the right and made for the less grand, although still impressive, St James Palace. We passed the front entrance and walked through the stables to enter the Palace by a side door. It was quite dark inside, but candles were burning giving off a rather pungent smell. We climbed a narrow staircase and entered a small room with two chairs in the centre facing each other. Behind them was a rather attractive day bed in royal colours. Kerr told me to wait there and that His Majesty would arrive soon. He gave me a smile and took his leave.

I looked around the room but there was not much to see. The walls and ceilings were white with no decoration on them. There was just a small grid in the wall, behind one of the chairs and a small window behind the other. I looked out of the window and could see the stables where the ostlers were tending to the horses. One horse appeared to be lame and it was being attended to by a blacksmith, who was hammering out a shoe.

I was uneasy about the grill on the wall behind me. Was it a voyeur's window through which a person behind could see the day bed? Was there someone there now looking at me? Could it be the King? Or was it just a grill where people could listen to a conversation which might incriminate the speaker?

I felt more and more uneasy. Maybe Robert Kerr was already there looking at me. I sat on the bed. It was extremely comfortable, far better than any I had experienced since arriving in Jacobean London. Better even than those at Wilton House or the one that Pembroke had provided for my cottage. I shuddered. Was this to be a real rendezvous? Was I to be compromised? Were things to happen, that I would need to eradicate from my memory and from my record? The cottage meetings weighed heavily upon me. What did the King want?

He arrived, wearing a long, beautifully embroidered day coat, with singlet and breeches and he was wearing immaculate shoes. He looked the part of a King, only of course, he wasn't wearing a crown. I immediately rose from the day bed and bowed. He put out his hand indicating that he wanted me to kneel and kiss it. I did so but he didn't withdraw his hand.

I remained kneeling, my head bowed towards the hand which remained steady. I could not see his face, only his slender fingers, his lower legs and his expensive shoes. He said nothing. Was he looking at me? At the window? At the day bed?

Eventually, he said, "You may rise Dr Fortune." So, I did. He smiled and pointed to the chair with its back to the window. He sat on the chair opposite. I sat down. In all of this ritual he had, of course, been demonstrating his importance, his superiority – and I thought his narrow-minded pride in himself as a powerful man.

"Jacob," he said, "Since we last met, I've had enquiries made about you and have been told by Cecil's men that they thought you were a woman disguised as a man. Can you believe that?"

"Yes, I can Your Majesty," I said, aiming to be totally honest. "My twin sister, in order to protect her sister-in-law, travelling to Oxford and then to Stratford, decided to dress as me, so that they would not be seen as too vulnerable women travelling together."

"Intriguing," the King replied, "As if they were characters from a play by Mr Shakespeare."

"Indeed, Your Majesty, I think that is how they got the idea, as her sister-in-law has helped to train the boys at that theatre."

"How do I know," the King said, "That you are not your sister?"

"Because," I replied immediately, "You have seen me naked."

"So I have Jacob," he said, "You promised me that no one else would know about that."

"I have kept my promise to this day," I replied, thinking to myself that I would expose him one day in my narrative. He, however, was not alert to my equivocation. I thought that my cottage experience might allow me to be forthright. "Your Majesty," I continued, "What is it that you want from me? Am I here to gratify your longings? Am I here to receive some punishment? Am I here to have, for let's say, 'an encounter', which will mean that I never speak about what has gone between us?" The King stood and so did I. Had I gone too far already? Had I said such forward things? He walked to the window and turned towards me.

"I want, Jacob, to know who I am beneath the spectacle and

authority of a King. You are a mind doctor, who can see into a person's soul."

I immediately corrected him. "That is not true. I can help you to see into your own mind if that is what you want."

"But can I say things to you that I can say to no other?" The King asked softly.

"I don't know Your Majesty. You may find someone else with whom you could share your most intimate thoughts. If you are asking me, as a psychotherapist, to listen to those matters which weigh heavily upon you, I am happy to do so, in confidence. But in doing so you would have to be honest, not just with me, but with yourself."

He indicated that we should sit on the day bed where he told me, in a nutshell, what he'd never confessed to his wife even though she had borne him plenty of children, some of which, sadly, had not survived. The truth was that although he was fond of her, he felt closer to her brother than he was to her. But then again, he knew nothing of women except for their childbearing and their witchcraft. He said he'd never even known his own mother, who was executed by her cousin the late Queen Elizabeth. He had been brought up by men in the Scottish Kirk. Scottish courtiers had always been his company, men not women. I remained silent throughout this. I'd been concerned that he'd brought me there to have some kind of self-gratification and certainly his display of power when he came into the room had pointed in that direction. But how could I move him on from talking about what I had suspected was his natural inclination to look for men rather than women? I decided he needed a little help and I sought it from the Bible.

"Do you think Your Majesty," I said, "That Jesus loved John the young disciple, who remained loyal to him to the end?"

"Of course, he did," the King replied.

"Then why can't you, as a King love a man as Jesus loved John or as King David loved Jonathan?" He considered for a moment and then sadly said that he had once done so. He spoke about his love for Esmé Stuart, the first Duke of Lennox, whom he had adored, but of whom the Kirk had disapproved. They had imprisoned the King as a young man, in Ruthven Castle for ten months, in order to break this infatuation. I asked him whether he meant the castle that belonged to the Gowrie family.

"Yes, of course I do," he replied. In his admission of this, it seemed that the Gowrie story had just become a lot more complex! In going back to the Gowrie's Castle, he certainly had a motive for revenge. Thank goodness the Master of the Revels had put an end to *The Tragedy of Gowrie*. It was a deeper matter for the King than the people of England had realised, but no wonder the Kirk didn't believe his story of self-defence. The King told me, however, that at that time, Esmé had been forced to go to France with his family, so there was no further contact until he died. Then his heart was brought back to Scotland, with a request that the Scottish King would look after Esme's children. This he had done.

"So why did you want to talk to me about all of this?" I asked.

"Because," he said, "I had been attracted to you at Wilton House, in that little cottage."

"But that wasn't attraction," I said, "That was curiosity, because of my colour."

He smiled and so did I. He then asked chillingly,

"How long do you wish to remain in my kingdom, Jacob?"

I replied, "Only as long as I can be of help to you, Your Majesty." I looked towards the grill and continued, "There may be someone else to whom you are now attracted. If so, be honest with yourself."

I learned later, of course, that the King was to enjoy a long relationship with Kerr, which would last for around five years before Kerr married Frances Howard.

The Scottish King looked at me with sad eyes.

"You know Jacob that I have condemned relationships

between men and find no excuse for it in anyone, not even myself." It was the first time that I had felt any sympathy for this deeply troubled man.

"I understand," I said and smiled. At that point, the King pressed my hand, stood and nodded. He left the room without expecting me to stand, bow or even leave his company before him.

CHAPTER 46

After a while, young Robert Kerr returned. He was to accompany me back to the consulting room. He refused to confirm or deny that he had been privy to the conversation. There were crowds pushing and shoving us as we approached the prison quarters. I asked what was happening.

"They are going to an execution," he replied. I inquired further and was told that it was to be of two men who had been behaving with each other in a way that the law did not allow. I asked Kerr what he thought about that. "Sadly," he said, "I have no comment. But I advise you Dr Fortune, to take care and return to wherever you've come from as soon as possible."

He looked me straight in the eye and said, "However much, Doctor Fortune, you may condemn His Majesty for hypocrisy and pride, remember that you were made welcome in a land that is no longer at war with Spain or France or any other nation. It is just that His Majesty wants to be liked and he tries to satisfy his God and his country. In doing that, no doubt he hurts many."

"You are a clever man," I replied. "I will think about what

you have said. On this, you have my word." With that, he shook hands and he left me at the door of the consulting room.

The King had confessed much to me and Kerr had kindly warned me that I needed to leave immediately. I knew the King to be fickle, so he might now decide that I knew too much and that I was a danger to him. If a danger to him, I would be a danger to his reign and his country. If that were to happen, I had no doubt that he would silence me!

As soon as I entered my consulting room, I found a note from Jackie and Ever, saying they had arrived and had immediately returned to the 21st century to be with Amelia. They begged me to join them, as for them, at least, there was little more to learn from being in Jacobean London. I pulled the cupboard away from the wall, lifted the mat and flagstone and removed my papers. But where was Spikey? He was nowhere to be seen. I could hear people outside. There was a knocking at my door. I set my coordinates.

"Spikey," I cried, "Where are you?" The door broke open as I vanished out of sight from the intruders, like witches at an execution.

I arrived back at *4 Psychotherapists 4 U* in somewhat of a daze. Amelia, Jackie, Ever, Dafydd, Maddy and little Angela were there to greet me. But how could I have left Spikey behind?

"You haven't," Amelia said as she hugged me. "Jackie brought him back." She pointed to where I saw him peeping out from underneath a cupboard. He immediately came to me, tail erect and purring softly.

We spent the evening talking about Shakespeare, Mr W.H., the superstitions, the witches, Macbeth, the Scottish King and life in Jacobean England.

My quest to some extent had borne fruit. The origin of the theatrical superstition had been identified. The quandary over Mr W.H. had been redefined as a deliberately constructed enigma. The nature of the play *Macbeth* had been clarified by the dramatist, mirroring life as an equivocal experience in which contradictions abounded in a world where, often

'Fair is foul, and foul is fair.'

ACKNOWLEDGEMENTS

Neither this book nor its prequel *Hamlet and the Psychotherapist* could have been written or published without the help and constant encouragement of Maggie, my wife. That is a simple matter of fact and I'm eternally grateful to her for that and her love.

I'm grateful also to those who kindly read the typescripts of this and the prequel: Michael Collins, John Drakakis, Margaret Kennedy, Cheryl Furniss, Durell Barnes, Marilyn Pugsley, John Pugsley, Laura Lees and Clare Asquith. I am also grateful to John and Leigh Spiers, my publishers, who took a gamble with these quirky novels, and to Andrew Chapman. Similarly, my thanks go to various psychologists /psychotherapists who have given me guidance about my writing, including Maggie Scott, Susan Elkington, and Pippa Hockton.

Any fault I acknowledge as my own.

BOOK REFERENCES

Although this story refers to historical figures it is a work of fiction drawing on years of studying and teaching the literature and theatre of the period. I am therefore indebted to the scholarship of numerous scholars and practitioners, whose works I have read or seen on the stage. Below I name a number of books which have been directly helpful, but there are many other writers and scholars, not mentioned, to whom I offer my thanks for their work and guidance beyond the books named here.

Bate, Jonathan and Rasmussen, Eric. *William Shakespeare's Complete Works* (2007)

Bearman, Robert. *Shakespeare's Money* (2016 / 2018)

Briggs, Julia. *This Stage-Play World: Texts and Contexts 1580-1825* (1997)

Clark, Sandra and Mason, Pamela. *Introduction, Macbeth* Arden Edition (2015 / 2021)

Coleman, Keith. *James l The King Who United Scotland and England* (2023)

Davies, Callan. *What is a Playhouse: England at Play* (1520 -1620) (2022)

Davison, Peter. (ed) *"Touring" Introduction, The First Quarto of King Richard lll* (1996)

Dillon, Janette. *The Cambridge Introduction to Early Modern Theatre* (2006 / 09)

Donaldson, Ian. *Ben Jonson, A Life* (2011)

Drakakis, John. *Shakespeare's Resources* (2021)

Duncan-Jones, Katherine. *Shakespeare's Sonnets* (1997 / 2007)

Duncan-Jones, Katherine. *Ungentle Shakespeare: Scenes from a Life* (2001)

Eagleton, Terry. *On Evil* (2010)

Moghaddam, Fathali. M. *Shakespeare and the Experimental Psychologist* (2021)

Finkelpearl, Philip J. *John Marston of the Middle Temple (*1969)

Greer, Germaine. *Shakespeare's Wife* (2007)

Greenblatt, Stephen. *Tyrant: Shakespeare on Power (2018)*

Karim-Cooper, F. and Stern, T. *Shakespeare, Theatres and the Effects of Performance* (2013 / 2014)

Karim-Cooper, F. *The Great White Bard. Shakespeare, Race and the Future* (2023)

Kewes, Paulina and McRae, Andrew. (eds) *Stuart Succession: Moments and Transformations.* (2019)

McIntyre, Ian. *Garrick* (1999)

Matusiak, John. *James l Scotland's King of England* (2015 / 2018)

Mortimer, Ian. *The Time Traveller's Guide to Elizabethan England* (2012 / 2013)

Nicholl, Charles. *The Lodger, Shakespeare on Silver Street.* (2007 / 2008)

Orlin, Lena Cowen. *The Private Life of William Shakespeare* (2021)

Porter, Stephen. *Shakespeare's London: Everyday Life in London 1580 -1616* (2011)

Shapiro, James. *1599 A Year in the Life of William Shakespeare.* (2005)

BOOK REFERENCES

Shapiro, James. *1606 William Shakespeare and the Year of Lear* (2015)

Schoenbaum, S. *William Shakespeare: A Compact Documentary Life* (1977)

Stern, Tiffany. *Documents and Performance in Early Modern England* (2009 / 2012)

Stewart, Allen. *The Cradle King: A Life of James VI and I* (2003 / 4)

Tanitch, Robert. *London Stage in the Nineteenth Century* (2010)

Taylor, G; Jowett, J; Bourus, T; Edgar, G. *The New Oxford Shakespeare* (2016 / 2017)

Thomas, David. *A Visitor's Guide to Shakespeare's London* (2016)

Wells, Stanley. *What Was Shakespeare Really Like?* (2023)

Wiles, David. *Shakespeare's Clown* (1997 / 1998)

Wood, Michael. *In Search of Shakespeare* (2003 / 2005)

www.ingramcontent.com/pod-product-compliance
Lightning Source LLC
Chambersburg PA
CBHW070910180626
46817CB00003B/994